DISREGARDED
AND *Adored*

THE WIDOWER'S PERFECT MATCH

BY
BREE WOLF

Disregarded & Adored-The Widower's Perfect Match

by Bree Wolf

This is a work of fiction. Names, characters, businesses, places, brands, media, events and incidents are either the products of the author's imagination or used in a fictitious manner.

Any resemblance to actual persons, living or dead, or actual events is purely coincidental.

Cover Art by Victoria Cooper
Copyright © 2021 Bree Wolf

E-Book ISBN: 978-3-96482-070-9
Paperback ISN: 978-3-96482-071-6
Hardcover ISBN: 978-3-96482-072-3

www.breewolf.com

Also By Bree

Love's Second Chance Series

Love's Second Chance Series: Tales of Lords & Ladies

Ignored & Treasured - The Duke's Bookish Bride (*Prequel*)

#1 Forgotten & Remembered - The Duke's Late Wife

#2 Cursed & Cherished - The Duke's Wilful Wife

#3 Abandoned & Protected - The Marquis' Tenacious Wife

#4 Betrayed & Blessed - The Viscount's Shrewd Wife

#5 Deceived & Honoured - The Baron's Vexing Wife

#6 Sacrificed & Reclaimed - The Soldier's Daring Widow

#7 Destroyed & Restored - The Baron's Courageous Wife

Love's Second Chance Series: Tales of Damsels & Knights

#1 Despised & Desired - The Marquess' Passionate Wife

#2 Ruined & Redeemed - The Earl's Fallen Wife

#3 Condemned & Admired - The Earl's Cunning Wife

#4 Trapped & Liberated - The Privateer's Bold Beloved

#5 Oppressed & Empowered - The Viscount's Capable Wife

#6 Scorned & Craved - The Frenchman's Lionhearted Wife

#7 Disregarded & Adored - The Widower's Perfect March

Love's Second Chance Series: Highland Tales

#1 Tamed & Unleashed - The Highlander's Vivacious Wife

#2 Dared & Kissed - The Scotsman's Yuletide Bride

#3 Banished & Welcomed - The Laird's Reckless Wife

#4 Haunted & Revered - The Scotsman's Destined Love

#5 Fooled & Enlightened - The Englishman's Scottish Wife

A Forbidden Love Novella Series

The Spinster (*Prequel*)

#1 The Wrong Brother

#2 A Brilliant Rose

#3 The Forgotten Wife

#4 An Unwelcome Proposal

#5 Rules to Be Broken

#6 Hearts to Be Mended

#7 Winning her Hand

#8 Conquering her Heart

Happy Ever Regency Series

#1 How To Wake A Sleeping Lady

#2 How To Tame A Beastly Lord

#3 How To Climb A Lady's Tower

#4 How To Steal A Thief's Heart

#5 How to Turn a Frog into a Prince

#6 How to Return a Lady's Slipper

#7 How to Live Happyily Ever After

The Wickertons in Love Series

Once Upon a Kiss Gone Horribly Wrong (*Prequel*)

#1 Once Upon a Devilishly Enchanting Kiss

#2 Once Upon a Temptingly Ruinous Kiss

#3 Once Upon an Irritatingly Magical Kiss

#4 Once Upon a Devastatingly Sweet Kiss

DISREGARDED
AND
Adored

Prologue

La Roche-sur-Mer, France 1812 (or a variation thereof)

A few months earlier

Elaine Winters, Viscountess Silcox, could not recall ever having been happier than when she found herself standing in the lush gardens of the Duret home in France amongst a sea of friends and family, old and new alike, and watched her daughter Juliet marry the man she had loved and longed for for over four years.

Henri Duret.

Happy endings were not impossible, it would seem. They did come to pass...at least for Juliet.

Seeing her daughter's joyous face, Elaine sighed, relieved that after all the tumult that had marked Juliet's life, she was finally happy.

Happy and in love.

Beautiful ribbons decorated the garden and a large table had been set up, heaped with mountains of delicious-smelling food. Children were running around, laughing and giggling, stealing treats and playing catch and pushing each other on the swing that had been tied to a thick branch of an old oak tree. Everyone was dressed in bright, cheerful colors, and merry voices mingled with the soft notes of a small musical ensemble situated on the eastern side of the terrace. Elaine felt a balmy breeze tug on her mostly chestnut brown curls—a few gray hairs were showing—as it blew inland from the sea barely a stone's throw away.

It was a beautiful moment. One Elaine would never forget. Yet she could not help the soft pinch that came to her heart as her eyes swept over the many smiling faces, for most were not simply happy...but in love.

An emotion Elaine had never known herself. Certainly, she had loved her parents. She loved her younger sister and, of course, her children. She knew love, but she had never been *in love*.

A wistful sigh left Elaine's lips as she watched her daughter sink into her new husband's arms. Juliet's eyes glowed in a way that brought joy to Elaine's heart...but it also stirred pangs of envy. If only she could snuff them out!

Even though Elaine's first husband and Juliet's father, Lord Goswick, had been a kind man, he had lost his heart long before she had met him to a habit that had seen them all but ruined. And then he had passed away, his life of gambling and drinking suddenly at an end, leaving Elaine and their young daughter alone to fend off debtors.

In desperate need, Elaine had married for a second time, accepting Lord Silcox's proposal because there simply had been no other way. Unlike her first husband, Lord Silcox had been a rather unfeeling man. An heir had been all he had wanted from her, and once she had given him a son, Jacob—or Jake, as they liked to call him—they had all but lived separate lives.

An arrangement that had suited Elaine just fine.

"Would you like a refreshment?"

Elaine flinched at the sound of her son's voice, her hand flying to her chest as she felt her heart skip a beat before it resumed its normal rhythm. "Jake, oh, you caught me off guard, darling. What did you say?"

Her son's dark eyes seemed to narrow in such a deeply concerned way that he looked far older than his twelve years. "Would you like a refreshment, Mother?"

Brushing a stray curl of his brown hair from his forehead, Elaine smiled at him. "Thank you, dear. I'm perfectly content. Go and enjoy yourself." Her eyes swept over the wedding party. "With England and France still at war, it will be a while before we'll get a chance to come together again."

For a moment longer, Jake's gaze remained upon her, something hesitant in his gaze, before he nodded and then returned to pushing his...?—yes, his step-cousin Antoinette upon the swing.

Indeed, their familial relations were somewhat complicated, which was precisely why Elaine only need turn her head to spot her second husband's first wife, Alexandra Winters, dancing upon the terrace with her second husband, Antoine, another member of the Duret family. Indeed, years ago, Alexandra had faked her death and run away from her husband in the middle of the night, taking their daughter Violet with her. She had been deeply unhappy in her marriage to Lord Silcox —something Elaine could understand—and when Fate had led her into the arms of a French privateer one night, she had given up everything for her chance at love.

And it had ended happily.

Again, Elaine sighed with joy and that familiar pang of envy alike. Alexandra had found a new family and a new home in France while her husband, Lord Silcox, believing her dead, had sought himself a new wife in Elaine.

Of course, the secret had eventually come out as these kinds of things always did. Fortunately, Lord Silcox had been the only one to learn the truth; however, afraid to lose his heir—as his marriage to Elaine was now void—he had done his utmost to eliminate the threat to the continuation of his lineage, namely his first wife and daughter.

With the interference of the Duret family, however, everything had turned out well, with Lord Silcox the only one who had not survived the confrontation.

Elaine had not shed a single tear for her second husband. He had been a cold and unfeeling man, and she was only slightly ashamed to feel relief at the thought of being rid of him.

Now, she was free and safe and master of her own fate for the first time in her life. Her daughter was happily married, and her son would grow up without the harmful influence of the man who had fathered him, but who had never truly been a father to him in all those years.

Life was good again, was it not?

Elaine knew it to be so; yet when her gaze once more wandered from Juliet and Henri to other couples in love—there seemed to be too many to count!—she could not suppress that sigh of longing that made her feel as though something was missing.

"I'm happy," Elaine whispered to the wind as it brushed over her skin. "Truly, I am." And she was in so many ways...but one.

And now, it was too late. Now, she was an old woman, and love was no longer something within reach. It seemed it had never been meant for her. Few married for love. Elaine knew that. She knew that her daughter had found something rare. And yet as Elaine looked around, her eyes seeing signs of love wherever they turned, she could not help but wonder, "What might it feel like?"

Unfortunately, she would never know.

Chapter One

A MOST PUZZLING NOTE

Errington Hall, England 1812 (or a variation thereof)

A few months later

Rather dumbfounded, Gilbert Stirling, Earl of Errington, stared at the small thank-you card in his hands. He was uncertain what baffled him more: the fact that it had been sent by a lady who had always rebuffed every attempt at a closer connection, or that she was thanking him for an invitation he had never issued.

"A Christmas house party," Gilbert mumbled under his breath, with his left hand stroking his salt-and-pepper beard thoughtfully while turning the card back and forth in his right, as though doing so would somehow explain this oddity.

Indeed, he could not recall when there had last been a Christmas house party at Errington Hall. With its old-world charm, it was certainly suited to it. Tall towers rose into the sky, the fortress's outer wall a reminder of times long ago when battles had been waged in the borderlands between England and Scotland. Tapestries depicting such scenes covered the brick walls on the inside while ivy obscured the ancient rock on the outside. An enormous fireplace sat in the great hall, a shield with the Errington coat of arms hung above it. Of course, Gilbert had ensured that the castle that had been in his family for generations was well maintained, every chamber comfortably furnished and equipped with the latest amenities.

With the card still in his hand, Gilbert stepped up to the window, allowing his gaze to sweep over the vast forests surrounding his home, now half-hidden under a thick layer of snow. "Where would she have gotten the idea that I—?" He paused, once more glancing down at the card. "This is not a mere misunderstanding," he mumbled to himself. "She writes in response to an invitation I never sent." Again, his thumb and forefinger traced the lines of his jaw, feeling the coarse hairs of his beard. "If I did not send it, then who did?"

In truth, there was only one other person who could have.

Striding from his study, Gilbert followed along the corridor framed by portraits on both sides. He crossed the great hall, his gaze momentarily drawn to the dancing flames in the grate, before he donned his winter coat and stepped outside into the crisp, wintry air.

The icy wind felt like pinpricks against his skin as he strode across the courtyard toward an outer tower that had served as a dungeon in times past. The heavy door stood open, and he stepped inside, allowing his eyes a moment to adjust to the dim interior. "Ethan!"

Out of the shadows, a scrawny boy of twelve years materialized, a wide grin upon his face. "You did not see me, Father, did you?"

Gilbert laughed and reached out to tousle his son's stark red hair. Ethan, however, darted out of reach with a triumphant glow in his blue eyes. "I did not," Gilbert admitted, once again taken aback by how quickly time had passed. It seemed only yesterday that his son had been only a tiny babe.

"I received a thank-you note from Lady Silcox," Gilbert said without preamble, his gaze fixed upon his son's face. "She writes that she and Jacob will be more than happy to join us here at Errington Hall for our Christmas house party." His brows rose in question.

Even in the dim light in the tower, Gilbert could see his son's face pale considerably. He seemed to freeze in place like water suddenly turned to ice, his blue gaze going wide as he stared at the card in Gilbert's hand.

"You invited her and her son," Gilbert surmised, needing no further confirmation. "In my name?" The last part was added with a bit of a questioning tone, for it would not do for Ethan to think it right to impersonate his father whenever it suited him.

Ethan swallowed hard, his mouth falling open as he searched for words.

"Why?" Gilbert asked, allowing a small smile to show upon his face. After all, he was not angry with his son. As an only child, Ethan often felt lonely when he returned home from school, wishing to have his best friend at his side as he explored the grounds and twisted pathways of Errington Hall.

Ethan shrugged his shoulders in a bit of a helpless gesture and then said, "I want Jake here for Christmas."

Gilbert exhaled a slow breath, then he placed a hand upon his son's shoulder. "You should have simply told me," he said in a stern voice that swung with understanding, nonetheless. "But why a house party?"

Again, Ethan shrugged. "Jake said his mother might not accept if she knew..."

Gilbert nodded knowingly. "That she would be the only guest?" He could not help but think that the lady disliked him. Why? Gilbert did not know.

Certainly, whenever their paths had crossed, Lady Silcox had spoken most kindly to him; however, she spoke most kindly to everyone. Never had it appeared as though she sought his presence or volunteered more than a polite conversation demanded. More than once, Gilbert had tried to lure her out of her shell; however, she had never taken the bait, a polite smile and a friendly word all she was willing to offer.

Ethan nodded, his blue eyes watchful as they looked up into his father's face. "Do you like her?"

Taken aback, Gilbert stared at his son. "What...what makes you ask that?" He cleared his throat, wondering if he had been too obvious in his efforts to further their acquaintance.

His son shrugged. "Sometimes you seem lonely." His blue eyes appeared wise beyond their years. "So does she, says Jake."

Gilbert blinked, then chuckled as a suspicion formed in his mind. "Are you two trying to play matchmaker?"

The serious expression vanished from Ethan's face, and a wide grin revealed two large front teeth that occasionally made him look like an over-sized rabbit.

Shaking his head at his son, Gilbert smiled. "You surprise me, my son. You surprise me." Again, he reached out a hand to tousle his son's hair, and this time, Ethan was not fast enough to duck out of the way.

"Will you let them come?" Ethan asked as he did his best to smooth out his curls. "Please!"

Sighing, Gilbert knew he could not deny his son's Christmas wish. He could not deny himself. After all, Ethan was right; Gilbert did like Lady Silcox, and perhaps this was the perfect occasion to find out if, perhaps, she could like him as well.

Gilbert held his son's gaze and then nodded.

Shouting with joy, Ethan jumped into the air. "Truly?"

"Yes, truly." It had been a long time since Gilbert had seen his son this happy.

Ethan's gaze caught on the card in Gilbert's hand, and a puzzled look came to his face. "What about the card? What will we say when they get here and there is no party?" His face scrunched up into a frown. "She will wonder why you did not clear up the..."

"Lie?" Gilbert supplied helpfully, one brow cocked.

Ethan's pale cheeks flushed red, matching his hair. "Yes," he croaked, an apologetic look coming to his eyes.

Pausing for a moment, Gilbert wondered why he had never thought of inviting Lady Silcox and her son. "I'll say the card was delayed and that by the time I received it, they had already been on their way."

With a rather blank expression upon his face, Ethan stared at his father. "That's a lie." His voice was breathless, and the look in his eyes suggested he was uncertain whether he had heard his father correctly.

Turning his eyes heavenward, Gilbert ran his thumb and forefinger along his jaw. Then he exhaled loudly and met Ethan's shocked gaze. "I won't say a word if you won't."

His son's wide gaze widened even more. Clearly, this was not Gilbert's greatest moment as a father. Perhaps he ought to reconsider.

"Yes!" Ethan suddenly exclaimed, and shock turned to joy as his eyes lit up with eager excitement. "Do you truly mean it, Father? Jake can come?"

Gilbert nodded. "Yes, Jake can come." And so would Lady Silcox.

Elaine, he believed, was her name.

As Ethan rushed outside, dancing and shouting with joy, Gilbert ran a hand through his hair, its once dark brown color now peppered with silvery strands. What had he done? Would this end in a disaster? What would Lady Silcox do once she found out the truth?

At least she was coming, Gilbert thought with a tentative smile, and perhaps he could make her stay.

For good.

Chapter Two

THE JOYS OF A MEMORY

"A house party?" Elaine's younger sister exclaimed with a frown as the two of them sat together in Elizabeth's drawing room over a welcome cup of hot tea.

Outside, snow fell in thick flakes, and Elaine was grateful that her sister's home lay on the way north to Errington Hall. The roads were treacherous and becoming more so with each day. More than once, Elaine had wished she had never accepted the invitation; however, Jake had begged her. She knew that he and Ethan had become close friends since starting school, and she had not had the heart to deny him.

"Yes, a house party," Elaine confirmed with a frown that matched her sister's. "Why are you asking?"

Elizabeth shrugged. "I've never heard of the Earl of Errington entertaining. That's all. I always thought the man rather liked his solitude up north in that drafty, old castle of his."

"Drafty?" A shiver snaked down Elaine's back at the thought of icy chambers and a chill in air that would settle in her bones and linger well into the new year.

Elizabeth laughed, waving a hand in dismissal. "Oh, I truly do not know, for I've never seen the place. As I said, Lord Errington does not entertain."

"How peculiar," Elaine remarked, wondering what had prompted the man to change his habit.

Upon the few occasions that they had spoken, he had not struck her as one to change his mind on a whim. His gray eyes always reminded her of the sea on a calm day, not a ripple disturbing the water. There was wisdom in them and kindness. She had never heard him raise his voice to anyone, his demeanor respectful and his manners impeccable.

Elaine had always appreciated that about him.

"Oh, I wish Hampton Park had a lake!" Elizabeth exclaimed all of a sudden as her gaze traveled to the window. "Do you remember how we used to go ice skating as children?"

A wide smile came to Elaine's face at the fond childhood memory. "Of course, I do." She grasped her sister's hand and gave it an affectionate squeeze. "It felt like flying, did it not?"

Elizabeth nodded, her warm brown eyes shining with wistful tears. "It was magical," she sighed before her gaze once more returned to the window, as though hoping that a heart-felt wish might make a frozen lake materialize on the grounds.

Elaine nodded, and with a sigh of her own, she surrendered to the memories that flooded her mind.

The scent of clean snow mingling with the fresh aroma of evergreens. The soft crunch beneath her boots as they had made their way to the lake behind their father's estate. The warmth of the sun upon her chilled skin as she had closed her eyes and savored the moment. Indeed, skating across the ice had felt like flying, free and unburdened. It had been a time before the confinements of life had forced Elaine to make choices she would rather have turned from.

"Errington Hall has a lake," came Elizabeth's voice, a suggestive tone in it.

Elaine blinked and turned to her sister. "You're not saying I—?"

"Why ever not?" Elizabeth asked with a shrug, something devilish lighting up her eyes. "Don't you think it would be fun?"

Elaine shook her head at her little sister. Even though they were both beyond forty years of age by now, Elizabeth would forever remain her *little sister*. "You forget, I'm an old woman. Fun like that is reserved for the young."

With a disapproving frown upon her face, Elizabeth scoffed. "Don't act, as though your life is over."

"I am not. I simply have more...worthwhile concerns at present."

Elizabeth eyed her with a disbelieving look in her eyes. "Would you care to enlighten me?" she challenged, lifting her teacup to her lips.

"I am a mother," Elaine huffed out.

"So am I," her sister interjected.

Undeterred, Elaine continued, "It is my utmost duty to ensure that my children are—"

"Juliet is married now herself," Elizabeth pointed out, "and Jake spends most of his time at school. He is growing up and needs his freedom to meet friends and explore who he is."

Elaine swallowed hard at the thought of the distance that had slowly come between her and her children in recent years. Yes, they were growing up. Juliet already had. In fact, she would be a mother soon herself, thus making Elaine a grandmother. "So?" she challenged her little sister. "That does not mean—"

"What about marriage?"

Elaine stilled as something cold gripped her heart. "You forget," she said, trying her utmost to swallow the sudden lump in her throat, "I *was* married. Twice."

A sly smile came to Elizabeth's face. "Some people say three times is the charm."

Chuckling, Elaine waved the thought away, trying her best to ignore the memories of her previous marriages. "I will not marry again."

Elizabeth sighed, then leaned forward and placed a hand upon Elaine's. "Twice, you married for reasons not your own." A small smile came to her lips. "Perhaps this time, you could marry for love."

For a long moment, Elaine simply stared at her sister, not knowing what to say. "Love is for the young," she finally replied, pulling her hand out from beneath her sister's before reaching for her teacup.

"That is nonsense!" Elizabeth huffed indignantly.

"Be that as it may," Elaine hastened on before her sister could be carried off into another lecture, "I accepted long ago that love is not meant for me." She swallowed, that sting of envy once more needling her heart. "Clearly, I am not...enough to tempt a man to fall in love with me." She forced a brave smile onto her face. "Perhaps it is for the best. I am freer now than I ever have been in either of my marriages. I like my life. I am happy, dear sister. Believe me."

That was a lie, and Elaine knew it.

Still, the thought of marriage brought on memories she would rather forget. Of course, not all marriages were the same. More than once had Elaine seen deep longing on her daughter's face when her new husband had drawn her into his arms. Elaine would never forget happening upon them by mere chance on her late-night stroll over the cliff top. The way Juliet and Henri had sunk into one another's arms would forever be imprinted upon Elaine's mind. It had been a moment that had made her wonder beyond all others.

Love was such a powerful, magical word. Everyone knew it. Everyone used it. But what did it mean? What did it feel like? Was it only felt in the deepest recesses of the heart? Or elsewhere as well?

Remembering the look in her daughter's eyes, Elaine had realized in that moment that Juliet knew the answer to these questions...

...while she, Elaine, did not. But she ought to, ought she not? She was the mother, after all.

"What about Lord Errington?" Elizabeth asked, jarring Elaine from her thoughts.

Swallowing, Elaine reached for her teacup once again, trying her best to hide her turbulent emotions. "Lord Errington? What about him?"

"He is a widower, is he not?" A teasing smile came to her little sister's face.

Elaine's heart stilled most disconcertingly. "You're not saying—"

"He might be a bit of a recluse," Elizabeth continued on, unde-terred, "but he is a most handsome man, would you not agree?"

Bright spots danced in front of Elaine's eyes as an image of Lord Errington formed in her mind.

"He is tall with those broad shoulders that make him seem like a towering giant," Elizabeth mused, that dreadfully suggestive tone in her voice once again. "And those silvery eyes of his!" She sighed almost longingly; her eyes fixed upon Elaine. "Have you ever looked into them? I mean, truly looked into them?" Another sigh. "They make a woman want to sink into his arms and stay there."

Elaine stared at her sister, a most unfamiliar feeling shooting through her. One, she did not care for. "Aren't you married?" she demanded in a voice that sounded almost harsh. "And happily so?"

Elizabeth grinned, something triumphant lighting up her eyes. "Are you blushing, dear sister?"

Gritting her teeth, Elaine willed herself to hold her sister's gaze. "I am not."

Elizabeth shrugged, as though they had merely been discussing the weather. "Then you must be feverish," she remarked innocently. "Perhaps you should cancel and remain here instead." Her brows rose in challenge.

A shuddering breath escaped Elaine's lips, and she was utterly surprised to realize that the thought of not traveling onward to Errington Hall displeased her greatly.

Why, she could not fathom.

Chapter Three

A MISUNDERSTANDING

The moment the carriage came rumbling up the snow-covered drive, Gilbert felt his heart almost beat out of his chest. He felt...young again. Like a schoolboy. Excitement pulsed in his veins, and he could barely keep still, eager for each second to pass, bringing them closer.

Bringing *her* closer.

And then the carriage drew to a halt, a footman jumped down into the snow, opened the door and lowered the step. Almost immediately, Jacob bounded out of the carriage, his dark eyes glowing, not unlike Ethan's. The two boys greeted each other eagerly, both their faces lighting up with thoughts of the adventures that lay ahead of them.

"I'm so glad you're finally here," Ethan exclaimed, slapping Jacob on the shoulder. "When we first spoke of this, I admit I did not imagine this would work." He turned his head and grinned at Gilbert.

Jacob laughed. "Neither did I." His grin matched his friend's as the two of them turned back toward the carriage.

Gilbert drew in a deep breath and then stepped forward to offer Lady Silcox his arm the moment she stepped down into the snow. She wore a dark blue woolen cloak with a fur-lined hood covering her head; still, a few loose strands of her chestnut tresses peeked out of the hood, as though curious about their new surroundings. Her eyes were wide, and she lifted her head, allowing her gaze to sweep over Errington Hall and its tall towers. Gilbert noticed her drawing in a shuddering breath—if from the cold or a sense of awe he did not know. "Welcome to Errington Hall, Lady Silcox."

At the sound of his voice, her eyes turned to meet his, and Gilbert was reminded of all the reasons he wanted to know her better. He was uncertain whether he could put into words all the different emotions he felt at that moment. All he knew was that he felt different with her nearby.

It was a simple fact; one he had been unable to shake or ignore for some time. If only she felt the same!

"Thank you for your kind invitation, my lord," Lady Silcox said with a polite smile, her manner reflecting every bit the gracious lady. She knew what was expected of her and fulfilled that role perfectly. Indeed, Gilbert could not tell whether she was truly glad to be here, to see him...

...or if she was merely being polite.

"Let us go inside," Gilbert suggested, knowing that there was more to say. "I am certain you wish to warm up after your long journey."

Lady Silcox nodded, and then they followed the two boys up the steps and into the great hall. A warm fire danced in the grate, and Gilbert offered his visitors a cup of tea as they all seated themselves in front of its glowing warmth. Evergreen garlands hung in archways and one lay draped over the mantel, Christmas ornaments settled within. "I must admit I was quite surprised to receive your invitation," Lady Silcox remarked, something curious sparking in her brown eyes as she accepted her cup of tea. "In fact, my sister, Lady Richford, remarked that you rarely entertain." The moment the words left her lips, her gaze fell from his and dropped to the cup in her hands.

Gilbert frowned, surprised to see that hint of fluster upon her face even if only for a split second. "Your sister is not wrong," he said with a sideways glance at the two boys, who had suddenly fallen quiet and were watching them with wide eyes. "I suppose there has been some kind of misunderstanding."

Lady Silcox frowned. "What do you mean?" She turned to look at her son, a questioning expression upon her face.

Gilbert cleared his throat as Ethan and Jacob seemed to grow smaller where they sat. "Frankly, there is no house party."

Lady Silcox's head whipped around, her eyes widening as they searched his face. "No house party? But..." Again, she looked at her son, then back to Gilbert. "But your invitation said..." Shaking her head, she frowned.

"I never sent that invitation," Gilbert told her truthfully, wondering what thoughts went through her head in this moment. "It seems that our sons wished to spend the holidays together and thought this *invitation* the only action to accomplish such a feat." He arched his brows meaningfully but carefully maintained the joyous expression upon his face. After all, it was the truth. He was glad that they were here.

Very glad!

Nevertheless, Lady Silcox's face paled. Shock widened her eyes before a mortified blush came to her cheeks. For another heartbeat or two, her gaze remained upon his, as though hoping that any moment he would reveal his words to have been in jest. When he did not, she surged to her feet. "Jacob, is this true? What did you do?"

Rising to his feet, Jacob met his mother's gaze, the expression upon his face slightly flustered, but determined. "I'm sorry, Mother. We did not mean to mislead you," he glanced at Ethan, "but we thought you'd never agree to this if you knew that—"

"If I knew what?" Lady Silcox demanded, anger hardening her voice. Still, her cheeks flashed a scarlet-red, and Gilbert knew she felt more mortified than angry.

The boys looked rather sheepishly at one another, then shrugged. Clearly, they had nothing else to say in their defense.

Slowly, Lady Silcox turned back around. "I'm deeply sorry, Lord Errington." The words rushed from her mouth as she wrung her hands, her gaze fleeting, as though she did not dare meet his eyes. "Of course, we'll leave immediately. We should never—"

"That will not be necessary," Gilbert interrupted. He took a step toward her, and her gaze snapped up to meet his. "You're more than welcome to stay."

For the first time, the lady's gaze lingered upon his, something contemplative coming to her eyes. "Did you know?" she finally asked, suspicion darkening her voice. Still, she did her utmost to remain civil.

Gilbert disliked the distrust in her tone, even though it was justi-fied...at least partly. "I found out when your thank-you note arrived. By then, however, it had been too late to set things right."

Exhaling deeply, Lady Silcox nodded, her gaze once more drifting from his, as though she did not dare look at him. It made her look almost timid, something Gilbert had never noticed about her before.

Casting a glance at the two boys, Gilbert then stepped toward her, and his voice dropped to a whisper. "I've already spoken to Ethan about misusing my seal; however, their deception came from a good place."

"A good place?" the lady inquired, doubt in her voice as she took a step back, clearly uncomfortable to have him standing so close to her.

Gilbert gritted his teeth. "They have grown close, as close as broth-ers. Is it not understandable that they wished to spend more time together?"

Lady Silcox cast a glance over her shoulder at the two young culprits. "They could have said something; instead, they chose to lie." Her eyes rose to meet Gilbert's, tension marking her expression. "I'm not...I mean, I wouldn't have...If Jacob had simply told me how dearly he wished to..." She swallowed. "I'm not a tyrant. I always take my son's wishes into consideration." She shook her head, pain lurking in her eyes. "Is this how he sees me? That he does not even dare—?"

Without thinking, Gilbert reached out and placed a comforting hand upon Lady Silcox's arm. "None of this has anything to do with you, my lady," Gilbert assured her. "Believe me, the boys simply loved the idea of an adventure, of planning this without their parents being any the wiser." He chuckled. "They want to be independent, make their own choices, be daring and bold. You are a wonderful mother to Jacob; after all, they went through with their plan, knowing they would be found out."

A small smile came to the lady's face. "Thank you for your kind-ness," she told him, then stepped away so his hand slid from her arm. "Nevertheless, I do not wish to impose—"

"You are not," Gilbert assured her quickly. "For years now, it has only been the two of us, Ethan and myself. We would be delighted to have you and Jacob here for Christmas this year. Clearly, the boys wish for it dearly." He searched her eyes. "Stay. Please."

Only a few steps away, Gilbert could sense the boys all but holding their breaths while Lady Silcox continued to look up at him, doubt in her eyes...and yet Gilbert could not help but think that at least a part of her wanted to stay. Why then did she hesitate?

"Are you certain?" came the lady's voice before she glanced past him at their sons.

Gilbert smiled at her. "I am. Please, will you stay with us?"

After another long moment that seemed to last a small eternity, Lady Silcox finally nodded. "Very well."

Loud cheers erupted from behind them as Jacob and Ethan embraced one another, then slapped each other's backs, congratulating themselves on a plan well-executed.

Although Lady Silcox cast them a stern and deeply disapproving look that silenced them instantly, Gilbert caught the small smile that tugged on her lips the moment she turned back to him.

"Are you truly angry with them?" he asked, leaning forward.

Sighing, she shook her head. "How can I be? You?"

Gilbert chuckled. "No, not truly."

"Do you think that makes us bad parents?" she asked abruptly, a slight frown upon her face. "Should we perhaps be more...?" Her voice trailed off, and she shrugged.

"There is nothing wrong with wanting one's child to be happy, is there?" Gilbert replied, enjoying this glimpse of a more vulnerable side of her.

Again, a smile that was not merely polite, but shone with genuine emotion, danced across her face. "I suppose not."

After Errington Hall's butler escorted Lady Silcox upstairs to one of the guest chambers, Gilbert turned to the boys, looking from Ethan to Jacob. "Well," was all he said, waiting to see what they would do.

Jacob's gaze narrowed slightly before his eyes darted to Ethan and then back to Gilbert. "You knew, didn't you, my lord?"

Gilbert laughed, exchanging a knowing look with his son.

"But you didn't give us away," Jacob remarked, frowning at his friend, as though hoping for an explanation. "Was my mother's thank-you card truly delayed?"

Gilbert shook his head. "It was not."

"Then why?" Again, Jacob's gaze moved to Ethan. "Why didn't you write to stop us from coming?" Despite the boy's question, Gilbert could not help but think that Jacob knew, or at least suspected, the true reason behind Gilbert's acquiescence.

A wide grin came to Ethan's face before he turned and whispered something in Jacob's ear, causing his eyes to open wide before the corners of his mouth stretched into a smile. "Truly?" he asked Ethan, before turning back to Gilbert. "Truly?"

Gilbert did not know what to say. Although he could guess what Ethan had told Jacob, he was not certain he wished to comment on it. "I am truly happy that the two of you are spending Christmas with us this year, yes."

"Come," Ethan exclaimed then, eagerness in his blue eyes as they turned to his friend. "I'll show you the dungeon. I'm certain a secret passageway leads there, and together, we shall succeed in discovering it." He pulled on Jacob's arm, who took a few steps before stopping in his tracks.

The boy turned back to look at Gilbert, something contemplative in his gaze. Then he straightened, squared his shoulders and set his jaw. "My mother is the kindest person I have ever known," he told Gilbert, a hint of warning in his voice. "She deserves to be treated with the utmost respect."

For a long moment, Gilbert merely stared at the boy, dumbfounded by the warning he had just issued. Then he nodded. "Of course." He held Jacob's gaze. "You're a good man, Lord Silcox." He inclined his head, pleased to see that not only youthful exuberance lived in Jacob's chest.

"Thank you," the boy replied before turning around and following Ethan out of the great hall, their voices echoing along the stone walls of the corridor.

Gilbert smiled, wondering what this Christmas season would bring.

Chapter Four

MEDDLESOME WORDS

Darkness had fallen over Errington Hall as they sat down to supper. It was a private affair, only the four of them, and yet Elaine felt as though she was sitting across from a stranger. Of course, she had spoken to Lord Errington countless times before, for they had crossed paths again and again because of their sons. They had spoken of school, their teachers, their studies. However, that had been the extent of their conversations.

"Are your chambers to your liking?" Lord Errington inquired as a footman placed a bowl of creamy soup in front of Elaine. "Is there anything else you require?"

"Not at all," Elaine replied with a careful look at their host. "The rooms are beautiful. Thank you."

Indeed, she had been most pleased to discover that Lord Errington's drafty, old castle was not drafty at all. A warm fire burned in every grate, tended to by most diligent servants. The stone floors were covered in lush carpets and tapestries adorned the walls, doing their part in keeping out the chill of the season. Her chamber was furnished in warm colors, reds and browns in various shades, giving the chamber a welcoming feel. Indeed, Elaine had felt persuaded to take a short nap after a maid had unpacked her trunks and left her alone that afternoon.

"I am glad to hear it," Lord Errington replied with a graceful nod.

Elaine offered him a quick smile, then equally quickly averted her gaze, hoping one of the boys would say something. However, both Ethan and Jacob seemed suspiciously quiet. Glancing in their direction, it surprised Elaine to see rather observant expressions upon their faces. Were they planning something else? Despite Lord Errington's reassurance, she did not quite like this side of her son.

It reminded her too much of his late father.

"This soup is delicious," Elaine stated simply to have something to say, anything to break the silence. It felt weighty and...odd, as though everyone was in on a secret.

Everyone but her.

Casting a careful glance at her host, Elaine almost spilled her soup. *Curse Elizabeth for her meddlesome notions!* Elaine could not recall that she had ever had any trouble meeting Lord Errington's gaze. Now, however, whenever she did, she could all but hear her sister's words echoing in her mind. *He is a most handsome man; would you not agree? And those silvery eyes of his! They make a woman want to sink into his arms and stay there.*

Yes, his eyes were a fairly unusual color. Elaine could not recall ever having met anyone with gray eyes, gray eyes that sparkled like diamonds upon occasion. Far too frequently for her taste! And now—thanks to Elizabeth!—whenever she happened to look into his eyes for a second too long, Elaine could feel herself becoming distracted, unfocused, her mind no longer able to uphold even a simple conversation. Why was that?

"Well, what plans do you two have for the next few weeks?" Lord Errington inquired, a teasing note in his voice as he looked from his son to hers.

Ethan's face instantly lit up. "We plan on discovering and documenting every single passageway of Errington Hall." Jacob nodded along in agreement. "As you know, I am certain that there must be one that leads out of the dungeon and I am—we are determined to find it." Again, Jacob nodded, a wide grin upon his face.

Elaine smiled. Indeed, Jacob looked happy, did he not? Perhaps she had been too harsh with him about misleading her. After all, he had merely wanted to spend time with his friend.

"That is quite an undertaking," Lord Errington remarked with a wide smile. "I wish you the best of luck. Where do you intend to start? In the dungeon?"

Both boys nodded. "We've already started," Jacob told them with barely concealed glee, "and we'll return to it the moment—" He broke off, a sheepish expression coming to his face.

Elaine rolled her eyes at him. "You mean, the moment you're released from our dreadful company?"

Ethan burst out laughing, then quickly covered his mouth with his hand. "Pardon me, my lady."

Relieved that she was no longer the only one upholding a conversation—aside from Lord Errington, of course!—Elaine smiled at him.

Unfortunately, the boys' impatience prompted Lord Errington to release them from the table before even dessert had been served. Instantly, they dashed away, leaving their two parents alone...

...and, in Elaine's case, at a loss for words.

"Are you all right?" Lord Errington inquired the moment their sons' thundering footsteps could no longer be heard. "You seem ill at ease. Is there anything I can do?"

Inhaling a deep breath, Elaine raised her eyes to his, once again overwhelmed by the odd sensations that crashed over her in that instant. What on earth was wrong with her? Lord Errington was merely her son's best friend's father! Nothing more!

"My lady?"

Realizing that she had yet to provide an answer, Elaine cleared her throat. "I'm fine," she croaked, then cleared her throat again and quickly averted her eyes.

Still, she could feel Lord Errington's gaze on her, sending shivers down her back. "You regret coming here," came his voice after another minute or two of painful silence.

Elaine's head snapped up. "No, not at all. I—" If only she knew what to say!

A kind smile rested upon his face as he watched her with those deeply unsettling eyes of his. Had he always looked at her thus? Or was it only her own state of mind that made her see him like this? "I assure you I am pleased to have you as our guests. Ethan is never happier than when he speaks of Jacob and their time at school. In fact, had I thought of it," he added with an amused chuckle, "I would have sent the invitation myself." He leaned forward almost imperceptibly. "Truly."

A welcoming warmth wrapped around Elaine, and she returned his kindness with a smile. "Yes, I've noticed their bond as well, and I am glad that Jacob has found such a good friend." She sighed. "Every once in a while, I wondered what it would have been like if he'd had a brother."

Lord Errington nodded, understanding in his gaze. "So have I." His eyes fell from hers briefly, a hint of sadness in them. "My wife passed a mere few hours after Ethan was born. She never even had the chance to hold him in her arms." He exhaled a painfully slow breath.

Elaine could all but feel his sorrow. After being fortunate enough to make a love match—as far as she had heard—his wife had been ripped from him in a moment that ought to have been one of the happiest in their lives. What did it feel like to lose someone one loved to such an extent? Elaine could not even imagine it.

"I am very sorry for your loss," she told him, displeased with her own words because they seemed to fall far short of the loss he had suffered.

Lord Errington nodded in acceptance of her condolences. "I am as well," he said then, surprising her. "I suppose it is difficult for a young man like Jacob to lose his father at such a young age."

Dropping her gaze, Elaine did not know how to reply. Somehow, it felt wrong simply to nod along and allow Lord Errington to believe that her late husband had been any kind of father to her son. In fact, she doubted that her husband had ever seen Jacob as a son, for she could not recall a single moment that he had looked upon their child with love.

"It still pains you to speak of him," Lord Errington remarked in a tight voice. "He must've been an exceptional father...and husband." His jaw seemed to tighten as he spoke the last word, as though the loss was his and not hers.

Elaine swallowed, knowing she could simply nod and be done with this conversation. Yet somehow, she could not bring herself to lie to

Lord Errington. Why was that? After all, they were barely acquaintances.

For a moment, Elaine closed her eyes, trying her best to collect her wits. She could feel the pulse hammering in her veins, confusion furrowing her brows, for she could not understand why she felt thus. "Truthfully," she said slowly lifting her gaze to look at Lord Errington, "my late husband only ever saw Jacob as an heir, not a son." Saying these words out loud twisted her heart painfully. Jacob deserved better!

Lord Errington watched her carefully as she spoke; however, when those last few words fell from her lips, his right brow rose ever so slightly, revealing his surprise. "I'm sorry," he replied in a soft voice. "Of course, I can only speak for myself; however, I believe fatherhood is the greatest gift that can be bestowed upon a man." A muscle in his jaw twitched. "Your late husband had to have been a fool not to have realized that."

Surprised, Elaine stared at her host, no longer feeling as though she were facing a stranger. "I've always thought so about motherhood as well," she finally admitted with a smile that felt good.

Returning it, Lord Errington nodded.

Elaine's gaze darted to the arched doorway through which the boys had disappeared. "Ethan is fortunate to have such a devoted father in his life. I can see that he adores you." Surprised by her own bold words, Elaine had to force herself to gaze at Lord Errington.

Lord Errington's gaze warmed. "The same can be said about you, my lady. Jacob is a remarkable young man, and it is clear that it has been your doing alone." He respectfully inclined his head to her.

Elaine could not help but stare at him. Never had anyone spoken to her thus, with such frankness, such simple honesty. "Thank you," she said, almost tripping over those two simple words.

"The late Lord Silcox," Lord Errington began, his eyes suddenly harder than before, "was he at least a good husband?" Something unspoken lingered in that question, adding a deeper meaning to it that Elaine could not make sense of.

At her host's bold question, Elaine felt herself blush, unable not to think of the few moments her husband had taken notice of her... namely to father the heir he had always desired. "I..." Although she would have liked to hide from Lord Errington's watchful gaze, Elaine's eyes rose to look at him. "I..."

His silver-gray eyes now possessed a darker quality, and she could not help but think that he had a personal interest in her answer. "Truthfully," he urged, as he held her gaze across the table.

Elaine swallowed, once again overcome by the desire to be honest with this man. "No," she finally admitted, feeling a great weight lifted off her heart at the admission. Although Elizabeth had always known how Elaine had felt about her second husband, even they had never spoken about it. "No, he was not."

Lord Errington inhaled a slow breath, as though needing a moment to calm himself. "I'm sorry to hear it. Clearly, the man was a fool in more ways than one." The look in his eyes told her that he meant every word.

Not knowing what to say, Elaine merely offered him a grateful smile. Indeed, this visit was not what she had expected...in more ways than one. Neither was her host. She had never thought about him beyond his role as Ethan's father. After tonight, however, she would be thinking about him.

Elaine was certain of it.

Curse her sister's meddlesome words!

Chapter Five

A LONGING HEART

Clothed in warm, fur-lined winter coats and heavy boots, Gilbert escorted Lady Silcox along the parapet wall. It was a cool, crisp day, and the sky was clear. "The Scottish border lies that way," he told her, pointing north across the snow-capped woods stretching far and wide. "It is barely more than a stone's throw."

"It is a breathtaking view," the lady exclaimed, awe ringing in her voice as her brown eyes swept over the land. "Did you grow up here?" Her gaze moved to him, lingered for barely a heartbeat, and then swept outward again.

Gilbert exhaled a slow breath, for whenever she looked at him that way, her lips curling into a tentative smile, he felt as though his heart might not possess the strength or perhaps the presence of mind to continue its rhythm. "I did, yes," he finally replied after she had chanced another look at him.

"It must have been wonderful," she whispered to the wind before her gaze caught movement down below in the courtyard. "There they are!" she exclaimed with a laugh, her gloved hand pointing toward one of the towers.

Gilbert chuckled as he moved to stand beside her, his elbow only a hair's breadth from where her own rested upon the old stone wall. "Ethan suspects a secret tunnel runs underneath this structure, all the way from the old dungeon into the main part of the castle." He turned to smile at her, momentarily mesmerized by the small cloud her breath formed in the icy air. "Lately, he has been speaking of little else."

Lady Silcox nodded, a wistful sigh leaving her lips as she looked down upon their sons as they rushed across the courtyard, careful not to slip upon the ice. "Since Ethan first spoke to Jake about his home," she turned to look at Gilbert, that tentative look back in her eyes, "he has been begging me for a visit." Again, she glanced at the two boys, now lying flat on their backs in the snow after losing their footing. "For him, this visit is a dream come true." Her smile grew deeper as she watched their sons laugh, then gather snow to throw at one another.

"Growing up here," Gilbert told her with a sideways glance, "I had brothers to keep me company. We inspired each other, were brave for each other and protected each other on our quests." He smiled at her as well as at the memories that found him. Then he shook his head, frowning. "Strange that I never realized how lonely Ethan had to feel with no one to stand by his side."

Lady Silcox nodded thoughtfully. "I grew up with a younger sister, and we did everything together. Even today, she is my greatest confidante. She knows me like no one else in the world." A laugh escaped her. "Sometimes better than I know myself." Her brown eyes met his. "It's frightening to have someone look at you and..." she inhaled an unsteady breath, "...and know what you're thinking before you yourself do." She swallowed and then abruptly dropped her gaze, returning it to Jacob and Ethan down in the courtyard.

"Are you all right?" Gilbert asked, confused by the way she had just turned from him, as though she did not dare meet his eyes. Had he said something to upset her? Or had it been a memory she had not expected?

"I'm fine," she replied as she had the night before, and once again, Gilbert thought the words were spoken too rushed to be truthful. He could see a slight tremble go through her and doubted it had anything to do with the cold.

"Would you rather go back inside?" Gilbert offered. "Perhaps a cup of tea will help warm you?"

For a moment, Lady Silcox hesitated, then she shook her head. "No, I'm not cold." Her eyes darted to him for a second. "If you don't mind, I'd rather stay. It is so...beautiful here. It reminds me of..." A heavy sigh left her lips.

"Of what?"

Her eyes closed as she lifted her face to the sun. "It reminds me of France." She chuckled. "I'm not standing up on a cliff and the sea does not stretch to the far horizon below my feet, but," she paused and turned to look at him, "it reminds me of France."

"Your daughter?" Gilbert asked, remembering what Ethan had told him. "She was recently married, was she not? And to a Frenchman," he added with feigned outrage.

Smiling, Lady Silcox nodded. "She was."

"And you miss her."

"So much," she exclaimed, hands now clutched to her chest, as though her heart truly pained her. "But I'm happy for her."

Gilbert saw the soft glow upon her face, the way her smile seemed to pulse with joy even though a hint of sadness lingered in her eyes. "She married for love."

The lady nodded. "She did." Her eyes seemed to mist with tears, but she quickly blinked them away, a determined smile curling up the corners of her mouth. "I could not have hoped for more. For years, I worried about her. I wanted her to be truly happy in her marriage and not—" She broke off, her gaze once more sweeping outward. "I always knew she loved him, but I never thought they would have a chance." She scoffed. "She an English lady. He a French privateer. Clearly, they were not meant for one another. In fact, they ought never even have crossed paths. And yet..." She shrugged.

"They did," Gilbert finished for her, hearing a deep longing in her voice. "You envy her."

As though slapped, Lady Silcox spun around, her brown eyes wide and her rosy cheeks suddenly white as a sheet. "I...I...never..." Her mouth opened and closed, her mind unable to express what twisted and turned in her heart.

Hoping he did not overstep, Gilbert reached out and placed a hand upon her upper arm. She flinched but did not pull away. Then he took a step closer, so the hem of her skirts brushed against the tip of his boots and waited until she lifted her eyes to his. "There is nothing wrong with the longing you feel," he said softly, mesmerized by the way her wide brown eyes looked into his. "You have every right to wish for love, for happiness."

"I *am* happy." Again, her words were spoken too fast to ring with truth. Indeed, it sounded as though she sought to convince herself rather than him.

"As a mother, yes," Gilbert pointed out, holding on to that fleeting connection he could sense between them. "But you were not as a wife." His brows rose meaningfully. "Nor as a woman."

Shock marked her features as she stared back at him, and Gilbert wondered if it had been put there by his boldness, or rather the realization that he was right. "I..." She swallowed, then blinked her eyes rapidly, as though trying to fight off a trance. "I should not have," she took a step back, and his hand fell from her arm, "spoken the way I did. It was most inappropriate." Again, she swallowed, her gaze once more distant, darting from the ground below their feet to the parapet wall and the courtyard below—anywhere but to him.

Gilbert tried to ignore the regret he felt at her retreat. "There is no need to apologize for the way you feel nor for speaking your mind." He waited, and after a long moment, her gaze finally returned to settle upon his. "We all need others to confide in." He moved toward her, careful not to step too close. "I loved my wife. She was the best friend I ever had." He exhaled a deep breath, surprised how difficult it was to speak the words out loud. "But I was never *in love* with her."

The world seemed to stand still as they stood up on the parapet, the clear blue sky above them and everything else hidden beneath a blanket of brilliantly white snow. Gilbert felt his lungs expand as he breathed in the crisp, cool air, his gaze fixed upon the lady standing only an arm's length away.

She, too, appeared startled into immobility. Her breath coming slow, little puffs rising into the wintry air, as she held his gaze, her own wide and revealing, as though a curtain had suddenly fallen from something she had always sought to hide.

"Father, come quick!" Ethan's excited voice cut through the stillness, making them both flinch. It was quickly followed by Jacob's. "Mother! Mother! Where are you? You must see this!"

The spell broke instantly, and Gilbert turned to see Jacob and Ethan stumbling out the tower's door and onto the parapet, their eyes lighting up the moment they beheld their parents.

Chapter Six

SECRET PASSAGEWAYS

*A*nd those silvery eyes of his! They make a woman want to sink into his arms and stay there. Oh, how right her sister had been!

Grateful for their sons' interference, Elaine took an unsteady step backward—away from Lord Errington and those compelling eyes of his!—before she could do something foolish...like sinking into his arms. Indeed, she had been tempted to, had she not? How was it she had never noticed the effect of those eyes before? Had she simply never *truly* looked at him?

But then, neither had he!

Elaine certainly could not recall him ever speaking to her with such frankness, such boldness, such... Oh, she did not even know what to call it. Whatever it was, it had created an intimacy between them that had made her feel comfortable enough to speak her mind the way she had.

As though he were her confidante.

Her friend.

Her...

"You must come!" Ethan exclaimed as the two boys came charging toward them, their eyes alight with eagerness. "We found another one! We found another one!"

Confused, Elaine asked, "Another what?"

"Another secret passageway, of course, Mother!" Jacob replied with impatience, grasping her hand and dragging her after Ethan and his father, who were already halfway back to the door, which led back down into one of the towers and the main castle.

Almost blindly, Elaine stumbled after the others, propelled onward by her son's insistent tug upon her arm. She tried to focus her mind on the here and now, but it was easily distracted by every look in Lord Errington's direction. What on earth had happened up there?

"Where are we headed?" came Lord Errington's voice up ahead, its warm timbre dancing down Elaine's back like a tantalizing shiver. Indeed, she could not recall it doing that before!

"The library!" Ethan exclaimed before the boys urged them around another corner and then down another corridor.

Eventually, they stepped into a vaulted room with tall windows and a fireplace almost as large as the one in the great hall. Heavy carpets covered the stone floor, and large shelves occupied most of the space aside from a comfortable seating arrangement facing the dancing flames in the grate. Evergreen garlands and even a sprig of mistletoe decorated the large chamber, red ribbons and straw figurines adding a bit of color here and there.

"It's over there," Jacob stated as he quickened his steps, pulling Elaine past the other two and toward a rather inconspicuous-looking part of the inner wall. "See the wood panel?" he asked with a grin, his gaze moving from her to Lord Errington.

"I do," their host replied, a chuckle in his voice that called to Elaine like a hail.

Lifting her gaze, she saw a carefully restrained smile upon his features as he diligently inspected the wooden panel. "Are you certain it is here?" he asked in a most serious tone; yet something sparked in his eyes as he spoke that...made Elaine realize he had known all along where the passageway was...

...but kept quiet to allow the boys their fun.

Indeed, had he not spoken of his brothers and him undertaking similar quests? Touched by his restraint and thoughtfulness, Elaine smiled, belatedly realizing that whenever his attention was not with the boys and their discovery, it lingered upon her.

Clearing her throat, Elaine turned to her son. "How does it work?"

With utter pride, the two boys explained where to push upon the wall—emitting an audible *click*—before the wood panel finally swung open, revealing a pitch-black tunnel leading off into nowhere.

"That is quite marvelous! Have you discovered where it leads?" Lord Errington asked, looking from Ethan to Jacob with questioning eyes.

Their sons looked at one another, their features marked by hesitation and something that reminded Elaine of the time Jacob had been afraid to sleep in the dark.

"May we come along as you explore it?" Lord Errington asked as he rubbed his hands together in a show of eager excitement. However, Elaine was certain that he only did so to ease the boys' fears as well as allow them to maintain their pride.

"Certainly," Ethan and Jacob exclaimed in unison, the strain upon their faces lifted as they went to light a candle before stepping into the darkened tunnel.

"Shall we?" Lord Errington asked as he offered Elaine his arm, a warm smile upon his face that tugged upon her heart.

"Of course," she agreed after a moment of hesitation, then reached out and tentatively placed her hand upon his arm, careful not to look at him as she did so.

"I promise I shall not let you fall," Lord Errington whispered as they stepped into the tunnel after their children.

Elaine did not know why, but she believed him. Oddly enough, if he had promised to show her the moon next, she would have believed him. Why, was a mystery!

Slowly, they made their way through the dark, the boys' candle the only source of light. The walls seemed rather smooth, the top curved into an arch, and the floor beneath their feet allowed them to move with little difficulty.

Only once did Elaine trip over a small imperfection under her feet, her fall prevented by Lord Errington's quick reflexes.

His other arm moved to catch her and pulled her back up before she even realized she had tripped. Still, her breath caught in her throat as she found herself pressed against him, his arms wrapped around her, holding her steady.

"Are you all right?" he whispered in the dark as the little light up ahead slowly moved away with each step their sons took.

Elaine swallowed; her hands braced against his chest as the dark slowly wrapped around them. Her first instinct had been to pull away. Her second, however...

Lord Errington's fingers grasped her chin, tilting her head up, trying to look into her eyes, which was near impossible in the dim tunnel. "Are you hurt?"

"I am not," Elaine whispered, feeling strangely bold. Perhaps it was the lack of light. Everything—including Lord Errington's enchanting eyes—were wrapped in darkness, and for a moment, Elaine wondered if perhaps...she truly ought to sink into his arms.

If a tree falls in a forest and no one is around to hear it, does it make a sound? Why that saying suddenly popped into her head, Elaine did not know...yet it made her push closer.

Lord Errington drew in a sharp breath, and then she felt the pad of his thumb brush over her lower lip, his fingers still lingering upon her chin.

Elaine's breath quickened as the world began to spin. She felt him leaning closer, as though...as though...

"Are you coming?"

Ethan's voice flung them apart as though burned. Elaine flinched as she felt the icy wall at her back, her ears picking up a muttered curse fly from Lord Errington's lips as he connected rather abruptly with the opposite one.

"We'll be right there!" Elaine called, trying her best to catch her breath. A moment later, Lord Errington's hand reached for hers, once more slipping it through the crook of his arm. Then they proceeded onward, not a word passing between them, as Elaine willed the heat burning in her cheeks to subside before they would step back out into the light.

Desperate to distract herself, Elaine counted their steps, relieved when the light at the end of the passageway grew and she could make out the outlines of the two boys beckoning them forward.

"It's a shelf that swings open," Ethan exclaimed as he stepped aside to allow them out of the tunnel. "See?"

Releasing Lord Errington's arm, Elaine stepped out into the room, careful to keep her gaze fixed on the shelf, which as a whole had swung forward into the drawing room.

"Isn't this marvelous?" Jacob exclaimed as he and Ethan slowly pushed the shelf back into place. It completely closed up the entry to the tunnel, once again blending into its surroundings, as though it were nothing but an ordinary shelf.

"Can it be opened from this side?" Ethan mumbled with a frown as he ran his hands over the smooth wood, no doubt looking for some sort of mechanism. Jacob quickly joined his friend, both their foreheads creased with lines of deepest concentration.

Disconcerted by the lack of communication, Elaine chanced a quick glance at Lord Errington and then moved closer to the shelf under the pretense of wishing to inspect it more closely. "Ethan, I cannot help but wonder why you have not stumbled upon this passageway before. With your curiosity, I would've thought you had discovered where all the passageways were long ago." She smiled at him warmly, relieved to have something to say that kept her attention focused on the boys and away from Lord Errington.

Ethan shrugged, a twitch of discomfort coming to his face. "Well... I've tried." His eyes flitted to her and then to Jacob. "One can easily get lost in this place, so it is far better to have another by one's side when one goes exploring." He straightened, clearly satisfied with his answer, then looked at his father. "Is that not so, Father?"

"It certainly is," Lord Errington agreed as he stepped forward and smiled at his son. Then his gaze shifted, and Elaine could all but feel it come to rest upon her. "Indeed, to have another by one's side is preferable in all kinds of situations. Would you not agree, my lady?"

To keep her hands from trembling, Elaine rubbed them together, pretending to fight off a chill. "I suppose that is true," she replied then, casting only a quick glance at Lord Errington. Still, the knowing smile that came to his face did not escape her notice. Was he aware of how deeply uncomfortable she felt? That he was the reason for it?

Still busy inspecting the shelf, the boys were completely oblivious to their parents. Elaine, however, felt goosebumps dance across her skin as Lord Errington slowly moved closer to her. He inhaled a slow breath as they stood shoulder to shoulder, his warmth chasing away the chill that continued to tease her with an unseen hand.

Elaine forced her chin up and then slowly turned to meet Lord Errington's gaze, determined not to let him see how much his close-ness unsettled her. Still, the moment his eyes looked into hers, all thoughts fled her mind and no words made it past her lips.

A corner of his mouth twitched, as though he knew precisely how she felt. Then he leaned closer, cast a quick glance at their sons, who were still busy inspecting the shelf, and whispered loud enough only for her to hear, "Your chamber holds the entrance to another secret passageway."

Elaine blinked, not having expected him to say that. "Pardon me?"

Lord Errington grinned at her, then moved another inch closer, and his voice dropped even farther. "I dare you to find it and follow where it leads." Something wicked sparked in his eyes for only a split second; yet Elaine had seen it, uncertain how it made her feel. What could be the meaning of this?

Chapter Seven
BEHIND THE CURTAIN

"May I call you Elaine?" Gilbert asked on their third day together as they once again walked along the parapet wall after their sons had disappeared somewhere in the castle.

The lady paused noticeably, and not only in her step. She seemed to still, as though considering his suggestion carefully, before lifting her head to meet his eyes. "I…I'm not certain that would be appropriate."

Gilbert had not expected her to simply agree to his proposition. "And who is to object?" he asked, lifting his brows in a daring gesture. After all, he was almost certain that her need to adhere to societal rules did not come from the conviction that it was the right thing to do but from habit alone. After all, it was the way she had been raised, the way she had always lived her life. While Gilbert had grown up in the same societal circle, he had spent many years far removed from society itself, and it had done him good. Out here at Errington Hall, he felt freer than he ever had in London.

The lady dropped her gaze. "It would set a bad example, would it not?" Slowly, her eyes rose to meet his once more. "Our sons would…" Her voice trailed off, and Gilbert could see that she could not truly think of a reason to refuse his request. Partly, perhaps, because she did not want to.

An icy wind swirled around them; yet the sun overhead shone

brightly, lessening the chill and giving warmth. "Would it truly make you feel uncomfortable if I called you Elaine?"

The moment her name fell from his lips, a smile claimed her face before she could prevent it. It instantly froze upon her face, though, and Gilbert saw a hint of mortification come to her eyes. Indeed, the lady was truly torn.

"Well?" Gilbert pressed gently, unwilling to drop the subject. He wanted to call her Elaine. He had *dreamed* of calling her Elaine.

Breathing in the chilled wintry air, she regarded him carefully, indecision still visible upon her face. "Only here?" she asked, her resolve wavering. "Only when we are...alone."

Gilbert could not deny that that last word had an almost intoxicating effect upon him, reminding him of the moment in the tunnel when she had lain in his arms. If only for a moment.

Slowly, Gilbert nodded his head. "Very well. Only when we are... alone." He leaned forward, held her gaze, and watched her draw in an unsteady breath. "Elaine."

Although she still looked uncomfortable, a hesitant smile slowly spread over her face. "Very well, Gilbert." Her voice shook a little, but she seemed pleased with herself.

Gilbert smiled. "Did you find the secret passageway in your chamber?" he asked abruptly, enjoying catching her off guard.

As expected, Elaine paused, her mouth opening, as though to respond. Then, however, she hesitated, thinking better of how to reply. "I did not look."

Laughing, Gilbert stepped in front of her, one arm leisurely draped across the stone wall. "Is that so? Come now, Elaine. Be truthful."

A youthful smile came to her face, and for once, she did not seem embarrassed at all. "Very well. I did," she admitted with a laugh.

"You could not find it?"

"I could not." She frowned. "Is it truly there?"

Gilbert nodded. "I swear it. I would not lie to you." Strictly speaking, he already had. However, it had been a small, almost insignificant lie, had it not? About her thank-you card and the time it had arrived? It had not been a true lie, had it? At least, Gilbert chose to believe so.

Elaine's face sobered. "I know," she said, to his surprise. Then she turned to look out at the woods beyond the outer wall, her gaze darting to him only briefly. "Where does it lead?"

Gilbert chuckled. "That you have to discover for yourself."

In reply, she cast him a disapproving look but said no more.

For a long time, they stood there in silence, the only sounds those carried to them by the wind. It was a peaceful silence, though, not strained and weighted by words unspoken or made uncomfortable by a lack of intimacy. Indeed, simply calling her by her given name made Gilbert feel closer to her.

As though she had given him her permission to step into her life and become a part of it.

"Your late wife," Elaine began without even glancing in his direction, "why did you marry her?"

Gilbert could not deny that he was utterly surprised that she would ask him such an intimate question. Thus far, she had always shied away from such topics.

Clearing his throat, Gilbert rested his elbows on the stone wall, his gaze moving to the far horizon where sky met land. "Because she was my friend," he finally said, remembering the day he had bound himself to Constance, "and because...it had been the right thing to do." He inhaled a deep breath, then turned to look at Elaine, her profile lit up by the sun in an almost ethereal way. "What reasons persuaded you into marriage?"

A heavy breath left her body, and her head fell forward as she contemplated how to answer him. "My first marriage was arranged by my parents. Our families had always been close and so it...made sense."

Gilbert nodded. "Did you love him?" he dared to ask, curious if she would answer.

For a moment, it did not seem she would. Then, however, she sighed. "I...liked him."

"Was he a good husband?"

"He was never...unfeeling or harsh," Elaine finally said, her gaze still distant, as though she was not speaking to him, but to herself.

Gilbert felt himself tense. "But your second husband was?" A growl rose deep in his throat, and he fought it down using every bit of restraint he possessed.

Her eyes closed, and he thought to see a dark memory pass over her face. Then she straightened and turned to meet his eyes. "I don't know why I told you all I have." She shook her head. "I shouldn't have. I should go." She made to step around him, but Gilbert moved in front of her, cutting off her escape.

"Did you ever love?"

Her head snapped up, and she stared at him with such an aghast look on her face, as though he had struck her. Yet something deeply vulnerable rested in her gaze, a longing she had suppressed for far too long. Tears collected in her eyes, and once again, her mouth opened and closed without a single word passing her lips.

"I'm sorry," Elaine finally mumbled as her eyes fell from his. "I have a headache. I need to lie down." Then she pushed past him and fled back inside.

Cursing himself, Gilbert rushed after her. He ought not have been so forward. Clearly, painful memories lived in her past.

Memories as well as regrets.

Still, some regrets could be helped. They could be silenced, alleviated and ultimately banished. That was precisely the reason Gilbert had not responded to her thank-you note sooner, in time for her to know not to come.

He had wanted her to come.

Because he, too, lived with regrets.

And only she could help him banish them from his life.

"Elaine!" he called as he rushed down the spiral stairs of the tower, surprised how quickly she had gained ground. He heard the echo of her footsteps, but he could not catch a glimpse of her. "Elaine! Wait!"

Stepping from the last step into the corridor, Gilbert finally spotted her, large strides carrying her away from him. Instantly, he quickened his pace. "Elaine, wait," he said loud enough for her to hear but not so loud that his voice would echo along the corridor. "I'm sorry I upset you. I assure you it was not my intention."

Perhaps it was his imagination, but her steps seemed to slow, allowing him to gain ground until he was close enough to reach out and grasp her arm.

Before he could, though, Elaine spun around to face him...and they collided.

Gilbert's arms shot forward to keep her from being knocked to the floor, gathering her against him as her head snapped up, her wide eyes staring into his. "I'm sorry," he whispered, knowing he ought to release her.

Again, they stood as close as they had in the dark passageway. Only this time, Gilbert could see a soft rosy glow come to her cheeks as her wide, brown eyes darted to his lips before she managed to avert them.

Deep inside, Gilbert smiled, rejoiced even because, despite everything, he had not been mistaken. He was not the only one who felt something when they were together.

"Release me," she whispered, her voice breathless as she chanced a look at him.

Gilbert released her; however, he did not step away.

Neither did she. "Perhaps it was a mistake to address each other by our given names," Elaine remarked, forced sternness in her voice as she lifted her head. "It only leads to temptations."

"Temptations?" Gilbert asked in surprise.

Elaine's eyes opened wide in shock. "Complications," she hastened to correct herself. "I meant to say complications." Still, a very becoming blush came to her cheeks.

"Are you tempted, Elaine?" Gilbert asked with a teasing grin as he dipped his head to try to look into her eyes. "Tempted to do what?"

Mortification stood on her face, clear as day. However, as she slowly began to back away, shaking her head, as though she could not believe what she had just said, Gilbert heard voices coming toward them.

Ethan and Jacob.

Elaine had to have heard them as well, for the expression upon her face became alarmed. Clearly, the thought of facing her son in this condition upset her deeply.

"Over here," Gilbert whispered and took her hand, pulling her behind a heavy curtain.

Again, they stood toe to toe, his arms around her, her back against the wall, as the dark, heavy fabric wrapped them into a world all their own. Gilbert had to admit he rather liked it. Indeed, this could not have gone any better if he had planned it.

"Sometimes I forget," Ethan mumbled as their footsteps slowly drew closer, "that you're already a viscount."

Jacob scoffed. "I know. I do as well. Nothing truly changed after my father died. I barely ever saw him anyhow."

With his gaze lowered to Elaine's, Gilbert watched her teeth sink into her lower lip as she listened. At her son's words, her eyes closed, pain and regret marking her features. For the moment, at least, she seemed to have forgotten that she stood in his arms.

"One day, you'll be an earl," Jacob remarked, his voice sounding as though the boys were on the same level with the curtain now.

"I never want to be an earl," Ethan replied, and Elaine's eyes opened, looking directly into Gilbert's.

"Why not?"

"Because it means my father will be gone," Ethan said in a forlorn voice that touched Gilbert's heart. "I'd rather not be an earl."

"I never cared for my father," Jacob admitted, a hint of anger coming to his voice, "and he never cared for me. He even said so."

"He did?"

"I was listening at the door when my mother pleaded with him to spend time with me," Jacob replied in a hard voice that clearly stated that he had never forgiven his father for his rejection.

Elaine's eyes closed once again, and this time, a silent tear slipped out and rolled down her cheek.

Without thinking, Gilbert reached out and brushed it away. At the feel of his thumb skimming over her cheek, Elaine's eyes flew open, and she drew in a sharp breath.

"I do not remember my mother," Ethan stated then, regret darkening his voice.

Their steps drew to a halt only a little way down the corridor from the curtain. "It would truly be great if our parents were to marry, would it not?" Jacob exclaimed with a little laugh.

At her son's words, Elaine's eyes widened, and Gilbert felt her body tense.

"Yes, it would be," Ethan agreed. "Where are they anyhow? I saw them on the wall a little while ago, but they have gone." The boys resumed their way down the corridor.

"Let's go look for them," Jacob suggested before their voices and steps slowly drifted away.

Elaine's breath came fast as she stared up at Gilbert. "I need to go," she whispered, utterly overwhelmed, her nerves in a wild flutter.

Gilbert nodded. "I know," he replied as he leaned closer, "but before you do..." Without saying another word, he swiftly dipped his head and kissed her.

And it felt as indescribable as he had known it would!

Chapter Eight

TEMPTATION & COMPLICATION

The moment Lord Errington—Gilbert!—kissed her, Elaine's heart threatened to beat out of her chest; yet a deeply peaceful sigh left her lips and she sank into his arms as she had feared she might.

And he held her.

With his strong arms and broad chest, Gilbert held her safely locked in his embrace. She felt one of his hands on the small of her back while the other held on to her chin, gently angling her head back before he deepened his kiss. His lips were teasing, coaxing, not forceful, but tempting in a way Elaine had never known.

Her first husband had occasionally pressed a kiss to her lips. That, however, had been the extent of it. It had not been unpleasant, but neither had Elaine enjoyed the touch. Her second husband had never seen any reason to kiss her—a fact for which Elaine had been grateful. He had wanted an heir, and kisses did not aid in accomplishing that feat.

Completely overwhelmed by the feel of Gilbert's mouth upon hers, the soft scratch of his beard against her skin, Elaine knew not what to do. She was an old woman by anyone's standards, and yet she did not know how—

Her breath faltered when his hand moved from her chin and gently, teasingly traced the line of her jaw before slipping into her hair. The pressure of his lips grew more pronounced, and a moment later, she felt the tip of his tongue trace the seam of her lips.

Elaine gasped. She certainly had not expected him t—!

When his tongue slipped into her mouth, her knees buckled.

Like claws, her hands curled into the fabric of his coat, heat shooting through her body. Perhaps it was the warm winter cloak she still wore! Perhaps...

Her thoughts became unfocused as she clung to him, allowing him to kiss her as he wished, marveling at the unfamiliar sensations that shot through her. She had not known she could feel like this. She had not known...

And then she felt him retreat.

His mouth pressed one last, lingering kiss to hers before he lifted his head. Even in the dim light behind the curtain, Gilbert's eyes shone silvery, the look upon his face watchful as he stepped back, his hands settling upon her waist—no doubt to keep her from keeling over. "I'm sorry," he whispered, a small smile tugging upon the corners of his mouth. "I couldn't resist the temptation."

Elaine drew in an unsteady breath, unable to catch a clear thought, much less express it. Her limbs trembled, and her heart beat so loud it felt deafening to her own ears.

Gilbert held her gaze for another heartbeat. Then he stepped away and held back the curtain, giving her room to leave.

To retreat from this moment that threatened to overwhelm her.

And Elaine did.

Quick steps carried her down the corridor and then up the stairs to the next floor and into her bedchamber. Once inside, she closed the door and leaned back against it, her eyes closed and her breath still coming fast.

Had this truly just happened? Or had she dreamed it? Had Gilbert Stirling, Earl of Errington, truly just kissed her?

Elaine could not help the smile that claimed her face in that moment, nor could she banish that feeling of utter bliss that spread into every fiber of her being. Indeed, he had.

And it had felt incredible!

Elaine spent the rest of the day replaying the moment behind the curtain in her mind. It made her blush and giggle, gasp and tremble. She sank onto her bed, then buried her head in the pillows, shaking her head at herself for acting like a foolish girl.

Yet that was how she felt! As much as she tried, she could not help it.

And then, a most disconcerting thought found her. "How am I to face him again?" Elaine whispered into the stillness of her chamber.

Only the mere thought of him made her cheeks flush hot with the memory of their kiss. How much worse would it be if she were to come face to face with him again? And, of course, she would! This was his home!

For a split second, Elaine felt tempted to pack her belongings and run, mortification getting the better of her. Then, however, she reminded herself that if she fled now, she would never feel like this again.

Of that, Elaine was certain.

If only she knew why he had kissed her. Temptation, he had said. Would he feel tempted to kiss her again?

In the coming days, Elaine barely managed to hold on to sanity. She felt like a fool. After all, at her age, she ought to possess the ability to comport herself with dignity in any situation. This one, however, seemed beyond her capabilities.

Once again, Elaine felt grateful for the presence of their sons, for she knew not what to say to Lord Errington.

Gilbert.

During meals, she kept her gaze fixed upon her plate and only spoke to the boys. When she spotted him in the great hall or down a corridor, she spun on her heel and hastened away. Yet, she wished to see him, wished to be close once again.

It was a most peculiar feeling.

And then, late one evening, about a sennight after their kiss, Elaine could not escape in time. Her foot caught on a corner of the carpet as she whirled around upon finding him in the library to which she had hoped to retreat in peace.

"Are you all right?" came Gilbert's voice, much closer than she would have thought. In the next instant, she felt his hand upon her arm as he drew closer.

Swallowing, Elaine lifted her gaze to his. "I'm fine," she croaked, cursing herself for behaving like a spineless ninny.

A slow smile spread over his face. "Our paths rarely seem to cross as of late," he surmised, amusement in his gaze as he watched her. "Also, you always appear to blush most profusely when our eyes meet."

Elaine felt ready to faint on the spot. Her hands shot to her face, and indeed, her cheeks felt hot. She had not even noticed!

Mortified, she pushed past him, but she got no farther than the door, for his hand upon her arm prevented her, pulling her back around to face him.

"Elaine, I'm sorry," he said with a contrite look upon his face. "I'm only teasing. I have no wish to embarrass you."

"But you did," Elaine replied, her voice harder than she would have thought and ringing with accusation.

Gilbert stilled, his gray eyes still watching her. "How so?" he dared her.

"I must go." Again, she whirled around, and again, his hand upon her arm stopped her.

"Why?" Gilbert demanded, pulling her closer, as the look in his eyes changed. "Do you not blush because the moment you see me, you think of nothing else but our kiss?"

Elaine closed her eyes, ashamed of the heat she felt surging into her cheeks once more.

"Did you not like it?" came Gilbert's voice, and when she opened her eyes, she could see tension marking his features. How could he believe she had not liked it?

"I did," Elaine admitted in a small voice, surprised how good it felt to say it out loud.

And to him.

"Then why do you run from me?"

Elaine shook her head. "I don't know."

Slowly, he moved closer, his gaze upon hers before it darted to her lips for a split second.

"Why?" Elaine gasped before he could kiss her again.

"Why what?" he murmured, and his breath fanned over her lips.

"Why did you kiss me?"

At that, Gilbert lifted his head, a frown upon his face. "Because I wanted to," he told her, confusion marking his features. "Why else?"

"Why else," Elaine echoed as her mind spun. She had never known it to do so; however, lately, her mind did so quite frequently. Namely, when Lord Errington—Gilbert!—was nearby.

"I need to tell you a secret."

Elaine blinked. "A secret?" Her gaze moved to his. "What do you mean?"

He cleared his throat. "When I received your thank-you to *my* invitation, there still would have been time to alert you to the boys' plan."

Confused, Elaine shook her head, her feet retreating a step. "You knew? You knew! Why then—?"

"Because I wanted you to come!" His answer rushed out in a deep breath, and he gritted his teeth, as though to calm the pulse Elaine could see thundering in his neck. "I wanted you to come."

"Why?"

"Why?" Again, he stared at her, as though she had asked him why he bothered to draw breath. A deep frown came to his face as he stepped toward her. "You truly do not know, do you?"

Of course, Elaine knew that gentlemen often had affairs, even mistresses, that even widows often tended to take lovers after their societal obligations to their late husbands had been fulfilled. Yet Elaine had never seen any reason to do so herself, nor had she ever received any offers.

At least, not that she had noticed. Had she truly been so blind? Was that what Lord Errington was referring to?

With her head spinning yet again, Elaine pushed past him and once again fled down the corridor.

Only the sanctuary of her chamber managed to calm her nerves at least a little; and yet, the chamber was his. She was in his home and would remain so until after the new year. What was she to do? She felt completely out of her element. As many years as she had spent on this earth, attending societal events, conversing with ladies and gentlemen alike and maneuvering her way through the torrents of life, Elaine felt

completely unprepared for...whatever it was Lord Errington—Gilbert!
—was suggesting.

Could be suggesting.

In truth, she still did not know what it was he *might* be suggesting.
Was it simply physical attraction? Or perhaps something deeper?
Either way, Elaine did not know how to handle her current predica-
ment. Never had life seemed more complicated than now.

Here.

At Errington Hall.

This Christmas season.

And then Elaine's eyes fell on a corner of her chamber she had seen
before but paid no attention to...until now.

It was a wood panel—nothing out of the ordinary—and yet it
suddenly reminded her of the one down in the library. She remembered how the boys had pushed upon its upper right-hand corner
before it had swung open.

For a long moment, Elaine stood and stared, Gilbert's voice
echoing in her ears. *Your chamber holds the entrance to another secret
passageway. I dare you to find it and follow where it leads.*

The memory of his voice, of the look in his eyes as he had spoken
those words, sent a tingle down Elaine's back and she shook herself.
Inhaling a deep breath, she took a step forward, determined to grasp
this distraction and allow it to chase all thoughts of Lord Errington—
Gilbert!—from her mind.

But could it? Truly? Had he not been the one to suggest exploring
this passageway...if indeed it was one?

Ignoring these nagging thoughts, Elaine carefully pushed the small
writing desk in front of the wood panel to the side, its legs scraping
softly over the floor. Then she moved around it and stood before the
panel, running her hands over its edges. It felt smooth, with carved
indentations here and there.

For a moment, Elaine felt like an explorer in a Mayan temple or an
Egyptian pyramid, seeking treasures beyond her wildest imagination.
The fire that burned in the grate cast eerie shadows over her chamber,
enhancing that feeling of otherworldliness she could not seem to
shake.

Oddly enough, she barely felt like the *old* Elaine in that moment, always proper, always in control, always dreaming...but nothing more.

Never daring.

Without thinking, Elaine gave the corner of the panel a soft push. She froze and her breath lodged in her throat when an equally soft *click* drifted to her ears.

"I cannot believe it," she whispered to herself as the panel slowly swung outward. A wide smile came to her face, and she felt her pulse racing with excitement. For a fleeting moment, Elaine wondered if she ought to alert the boys to her find; however, she quickly shook off that thought.

Not now. They were probably—hopefully!—already asleep and this —here and now—was *her* moment.

Hers alone.

Hurrying over to the fireplace, Elaine quickly lit the candle from her bedside table and then approached the dark, gaping hole in the corner of her chamber. Cool air teased her skin as she stepped up to the threshold, her eyes squinting, trying to see through the dark.

Then she hesitated, belatedly realizing that she was already in her nightgown, a woolen robe over it to fend off the night's cold. Ought she to change? Or perhaps leave the exploration of her find to the next day?

Deep inside her, something rebelled against the thought of staying behind, of retreating, of ignoring this moment that made her pulse beat wildly in her veins. No, this was *her* moment. Never had she been daring.

Never.

But she would be tonight.

No matter what, she would not retreat.

Breathing in deeply, hoping for a surge of courage to propel her forward, Elaine carefully set one foot into the dark tunnel.

And then another.

And another.

Slowly, she made her way down the pitch-black corridor, lifting her candle to see its smooth rock walls and arched ceiling. With each step, the chill in the tunnel settled deeper into her limbs, and she felt herself begin to shiver despite the woolen robe she wore. Still, she continued on, her eyes fixed on the end of the tunnel.

The end, she could not see.

Endless moments passed before her small light fell on another wall, this one not made of stone, but wood like the one she had come through. What would she find on the other side? Another guest chamber? A drawing room? Or perhaps even the dungeon?

The thought of accidentally stumbling upon the dungeon the boys longed to find made her smile, and she reached out a hand and gave the wooden panel a forceful push. Instantly, the door opened slowly, inch by inch, revealing another furnished chamber.

It, too, was illuminated by a warm fire as well as several lit sconces along the walls, shadows dancing here and there like separate entities. Entranced, Elaine stepped forward, belatedly realizing what that meant: the chamber was occupied.

"I see you found that secret passage after all," came Gilbert's voice a moment before he stepped around the panel and into her line of sight.

Elaine froze, her eyes going wide not merely because of his presence—or rather hers in his chamber!—but because he no longer wore the jacket and vest and necktie he had before. Indeed, his collar stood open, and he looked as though he was undressing for bed.

Instantly, heat shot into Elaine's cheeks and she spun on her heels to hasten back into the tunnel.

Chapter Nine

DARE TO BE DARING

Before Elaine could take a single step, Gilbert rushed forward, his hands reaching for her arms, pulling her back. With his boot, he kicked the panel closed, drawing her away from the passageway and toward the fire in his grate. "Come, warm yourself," he murmured softly, well-aware of the paleness of her skin and her wide-open eyes as they swept over his chamber. "The tunnels are freezing, especially this time of year." Ignoring her reluctance, Gilbert deposited her in front of the roaring fire before retrieving a blanket to drape upon her shoulders. "There. Better?"

Still staring at him, Elaine nodded, her candle still clutched in her hands. "This is your ch-chamber," she stammered, clearly mortified. Gilbert could tell that whatever she had expected to find at the end of this tunnel had not been him!

Gilbert chuckled. "It is," he confirmed, delighted that she had found the tunnel. After not discovering the passageway when he had first spoken to her of it, he had feared she would never try again.

But she had.

And now she was here.

Gilbert had secretly hoped for such a moment.

"Th-This is y-your ch-chamber?" she asked once more, the candle in her hands now shaking so badly that Gilbert feared it might topple to the floor.

Moving forward, Gilbert took it from her hands and set it on the mantel. "It is."

She eyed him with apprehension. "Your... Your bedchamber?"

Gilbert grinned at her, casting a quick glance over his shoulder at his bed. "So it would seem."

The paleness instantly vanished from her cheeks, replaced by the fetching blush he had come to expect and love. "And you're dressed in—" She broke off, her eyes sweeping over his form. "And I—" Her gaze moved down the length of her night robe before snapping back up. "I need to go."

Yet she stayed where she was, her eyes upon him, confusion marking her features.

Gilbert wished he knew what was going through her head at this moment. "I wish you'd stay."

She blinked, then swallowed. "You do? Why?" Again, her gaze swept over his chamber. "Why—?" She spoke up abruptly, then equally quickly broke off, her eyes hardening as she stared at him. "I...I expected to find a...a drawing room of some sort. Not..." While her left hand continued to hold on to the blanket upon her shoulders, her right swept outward, indicating his chamber.

Seeing her confusion, Gilbert chuckled, remembering how composed she had always appeared. However, even then, he had suspected—hoped, perhaps!—that it might only be a facade.

"Why would you give me a chamber," Elaine asked, indignation narrowing her eyes as she drew back her shoulders, "that is connected to yours through a secret passageway? This is most untoward! I—"

"Because I needed you to understand something," Gilbert interrupted her before her irritation could get the better of her.

Elaine blinked. "Understand what?" she asked after a moment of pause, as though she was uncertain whether she liked to know the answer.

Holding her gaze, Gilbert approached, slowly closing the remaining distance between them. He watched her most carefully as he moved, saw her tense at his approach, but she did not back away. And then he stood before her, and instead of explaining himself, he merely lifted his right forefinger and pointed upward.

Confusion flitted across her features before she raised her chin, her eyes moving to the ceiling. The moment she beheld the small sprig of mistletoe he knew to be there, her jaw dropped and her eyes snapped back to his. "What—? Why—?" She fixed him with a pointed stare. "You did this," she accused, pointing a finger at him. "You maneuvered me here! To this very spot! You maneuvered me here to—" She broke off, still staring at him.

Gilbert nodded. "I did," he admitted. "I wanted to kiss you again." At his admission, she blinked. "I *want* to kiss you again." He inched closer. "Does that surprise you?"

An unsteady breath rushed from her lungs as her mouth opened, then closed. "I..."

Understanding her perfectly, Gilbert moved without hesitation. His hands reached for her, and within a single heartbeat, she was in his arms, her head tilted upward to receive his kiss.

Trembling, she clung to him, her lips soft and yielding as he kissed her the way he had a sennight ago behind the curtain. Countless times he had replayed that moment in his mind, wishing for another. And now, here she was.

Growing bolder, Gilbert moved to untie the belt of her robe, his hands reaching underneath and settling onto her waist. He could feel her tremble, her hands tentative as they moved to his shoulders. She swayed slightly, and instantly, her hands tensed, digging into his flesh to keep herself upright.

Then she pulled back, her eyes wide as they looked into his. "We..." She swallowed. "We shouldn't." Shaking her head, she took a step back. "I shouldn't be here. We shouldn't..." She stared at him, and Gilbert could not shake the feeling that she was trying to convince herself to leave...

...but hoped to be unsuccessful.

Releasing his hold on her, Gilbert stepped back, not wishing to coax her into something she did not want. If she stayed with him tonight, he wanted her to want it as much as he did.

Yet her wide gaze remained upon his, as though she wished he would persuade her, offer her a reason that would allow her to stay.

"Here, in this room," Gilbert said softly, "we're not who we are out there." He nodded toward the door and all that lay beyond. "In here, in this moment, you are not a mother and I'm not a father. We're not Lady Silcox and Lord Errington." Seeing her exhale slowly, he smiled at her. "Right here, right now, we're simply Elaine and Gilbert. Nothing and no one else matters." He took a careful step toward her, mesmerized by the look in her eyes. "What do you want, Elaine?" He reached to grasp her hands and held them within his own. "You. What do *you* want? Here. Now. Do you wish to leave?" He squeezed her hands. "If you do, I'll escort you back to your chamber. I assure you."

Questions lingered in her wide eyes, and for a moment, Gilbert thought she would ask him what would happen if she did not wish to leave. "You planned this," Elaine said instead, a slight frown coming to her face, her eyes darting up to the sprig of mistletoe above their heads. "Why?"

Smiling, Gilbert exhaled a deep breath. "From the first moment I saw you," he whispered, slowly pulling her ever closer until no more space remained between them, "I knew I wanted to know you...in every possible way." She swallowed but did not retreat. "Yet you never noticed, did you?"

Slowly, Elaine shook her head, doubt in her eyes. "You wanted to know me?"

"Yes."

"Then why...? Why did you never say anything?" She shook her head again, the look of doubt intensifying. "If you...cared for me...in any way, how come...?"

"Because I thought you knew but did not reciprocate," Gilbert explained, remembering his frustration when he thought she was trying to tell him quite politely to bury his hopes. "Believe me, more than once, I was tempted to simply whisk you into my arms and kiss you."

Her jaw dropped slightly at his bold admission. "I had no idea," she gasped, almost breathless. "I...I didn't know."

"You do now." His arm wrapped around her middle, urging her closer, as he lowered his forehead to hers. "What do you want?"

Elaine's breath came fast as she looked up into his eyes. "I...I want..." She bit her lower lip, clearly not accustomed to contemplating that question.

Gilbert slid one hand to the back of her neck, his eyes searching hers. "Do you want me to return you to your chamber?" he whispered against her lips. "Or...?" He left the question unfinished and simply lowered his head, bridging the last remaining gap between them, and claimed her lips.

Would she pull away and leave him? Or would she stay?

Chapter Ten

A NIGHT TO REMEMBER

The moment Gilbert kissed her, all thoughts fled Elaine's mind and her heart seemed to swell to twice its size. Her skin hummed with delight at the soft touch of his fingertips, and her lips eagerly responded to his explorations.

Still, somewhere deep down, Elaine knew very well that she ought to stop him. More than that, she ought not participate. Indeed, it seemed her hands had a mind of their own. They reached higher and grasped his face, feeling the coarse hairs of his beard against her skin. She held him to her, kissing him back with equal fervor. Her own behavior would no doubt have shocked her witless had she been in her right mind. However, she could not possibly be. Perhaps she was suffering from some kind of temporary insanity? Was that possible?

Gilbert's hands moved to her shoulders, and she dimly registered that he was trying to remove her robe. The thought sent a rather unfamiliar thrill through her, and yet she did not hesitate to drop her arms and help him along in his efforts. The moment the garment fell to the floor, her hands once more reached for him, feeling his warm skin beneath her fingertips as she explored his open collar.

Indeed, if she were in her right mind, her face would be ablaze with mortification!

Gilbert chuckled against her lips, and for a moment, Elaine feared he had read her thoughts. "Last chance to reconsider," he murmured, then kissed her again without waiting for an answer. His arms wrapped around her in a way that she felt almost lifted off her feet.

A moment later, she was, for Gilbert scooped her up and held her safely in his arms, his lips never leaving hers. Then he moved toward the bed, and Elaine was surprised that she felt not a moment of unease, of indecision, of doubt.

Indeed, she wondered if this was the way Juliet felt in her husband's arms. If her daughter had learned the magic of such a moment before she, Elaine, had.

Better late than never, her mind counseled helpfully, warning her not to do something foolish but to enjoy this moment. After all, Elaine had made it through almost five decades without ever feeling like this, without ever knowing it to be possible.

Come hell or high water, she would not ruin this moment. This experience. Who knew if she would ever feel like this again?

And so, for once, Elaine allowed not a single doubt to rear its ugly head as she felt herself sink into Gilbert's downy soft mattress, his warm body all she needed to keep the cool air at bay.

Indeed, her instincts proved her right because it was a night like no other. Never could Elaine have imagined anything remotely like it. She hardly recognized herself, her thoughts and emotions foreign, as though belonging to another. The woman she could have been, perhaps? In another life?

Sometime during the night, Elaine woke with a start. She did not know why, but she was suddenly wide awake, and the moment the memory of what they had done here in this bed resurfaced, she surged upward, her eyes wide as they tried to see through the dim light.

Gilbert lay on his back beside her, one arm flung over his face, his chest rising and falling with even breaths.

For a few heartbeats, Elaine simply stared at him, her hand holding the blanket to her chest, for she was suddenly all too aware of her nakedness.

As well as his.

Instantly, the spell of the night slipped away. Mortification shot through her, and she felt her cheeks heat beyond compare. It seemed her devil-may-care attitude had simply evaporated, leaving her alone to face each and every consequence of her misstep. And it had been a misstep, had it not?

Glimpsing her night rail on the floor only a few feet away, Elaine silently slipped from the bed and quickly pulled it over her head. She found her slippers and then her robe where it lay near the fireplace. All the while, she cast almost fearful glances at the bed, wishing and fearing with equal measure Gilbert would wake.

But he did not.

And so Elaine retraced her steps, took the remainder of her candle from the mantel and then quietly opened the wooden panel that would lead her into the tunnel, which in turn would allow her to return to her own chamber with no one the wiser.

The moment the panel clicked shut behind her, her eyes falling on her own bed, Elaine breathed out deeply...if in relief or something else she could not say. Although she ought to sleep, she could not. Her limbs hummed with wakefulness, with energy, with...the desire to return to Gilbert.

Lord Errington.

Pacing the length of her chamber, Elaine paused and then buried her face in her hands. "What have I done?" she moaned, then bit her lip hard, welcoming the sharp pain as her wayward thoughts returned to the moments she had just experienced.

Indeed, it had never felt like that with either of her husbands. She had never once...enjoyed herself, their touch, the moment. She had never felt close to them despite the physical closeness necessary for the act.

But she had with Gilbert. But had he, as well?

Gripping the bottom right pole of her four-poster bed, Elaine leaned her forehead against its smooth wood and exhaled slowly. Why had Gilbert put her in this chamber? The one connected to his own through a secret passageway? Had he anticipated such a night? If so...

Elaine swallowed. "What now?" she whispered to the empty room. Had he spoken the truth? Did he truly care for her? Or had he simply said so in order to persuade her into his bed? Had she been a fool to believe him?

Although she was not a very worldly woman, Elaine was aware that all men had need of a woman every now and then, did they not? And Gilbert was a widower. Perhaps it had simply been a desire of the flesh and nothing more.

Closing her eyes, Elaine sighed, realizing in that moment that she wanted more. Yes, their encounter had been wonderful, and she was grateful to have at least experienced passion if not love; however, a part of her was far from happy with the thought that what they had shared this night had been the extent of his interest in her. Would he now no longer seek her out as he had? Would his ardor cool now that he had known her? Had she been a mere conquest for him?

Elaine had to admit that he had never once spoken to her of love. His words had been wonderful. They had made her feel precious; but they had been vague, had they not? Never once had his words suggested he might consider remarrying.

And even if he did...

Her fingers all but clawed into the wooden pole of her bed. "Would he still want me if he knew?" she whispered as her heart grew heavy, pain surging through it in a way she had never known.

Elaine doubted it very much.

Men of honor did not want to get mixed up with scandal. Of course, Elaine prayed that her secret would never be revealed, that no one would ever learn that her second marriage had never been valid, that her son was illegitimate, but she was no fool. She knew secrets like that often had a way of finding the light of day, no matter how hard one might try to hide them. Almost daily, she feared what might happen to her and, more importantly, to Jake if it became known that her late husband's first wife was still alive, that he had never been free to marry her, Elaine.

That their child was a bastard.

Elaine hated that word. How could it ever be a child's fault to be born out of wedlock? Why was the world so cruel as to punish the innocent?

Sinking down onto her bed, Elaine suddenly felt exhausted. Perhaps coming to Errington Hall had been a mistake. Perhaps she had been wrong to indulge herself in her desires. Perhaps it would be wise to leave as soon as possible.

At least she could take the memory of this night with her. At least, she would always have that.

No matter what happened.

Chapter Eleven

THE LIGHT OF DAY

Gilbert was surprised at the deep sense of disappointment he felt when he woke up alone that morning. Elaine's scent still lingered upon his pillow, yet her warmth had disappeared. It left him feeling chilled, and he felt a deep yearning to seek her out.

Unfortunately, she was not in her chamber when he knocked, and so he strode down to the breakfast parlor, relieved to see her seated at the table. To his utter astonishment, however, she did not even look up at his entrance, her eyes downcast and her posture tense.

"Good morning, Father," Ethan greeted him while Jacob offered him a very grown-up nod.

"Good morning." Striding around the table, Gilbert seated himself, his gaze traveling to the quiet woman to his left, who still refused to meet his eyes. If he did not know any better, he would think her completely unaware of his presence.

"Which chamber should we search next?" Ethan exclaimed, and his gaze moved from Jacob to his father. "So far, we've inspected the library, the kitchen, the downstairs drawing room, the stables, the dungeon itself and—"

"Do you truly think there is a tunnel that leads out of the dungeon?" Jacob asked with a disappointed frown. "Why would anyone even put it in there? Would that not assist prisoners in their escape?"

"One would think so," Ethan stated in a way that made Gilbert smile, his son's eloquent speech once again reminding him how much time had passed since he had been a babe. "In the library, I found an old journal. It did not have a name on it, but I'm certain it was written by one of our ancestors." He glanced at Gilbert. "In it, he mentions an escape from that very library during a fire, and from the way he wrote, he did not simply step out the door and move down the corridor."

Jacob frowned thoughtfully. "Do you think there are tunnels in every chamber? Perhaps we should search them all."

Out of the corner of his eye, Gilbert saw Elaine flinch before her gaze flickered to his for a split second. He could feel it like a punch to his gut, stealing the air from his lungs and drawing a groan from his lips.

"Are you all right, Father?" Ethan asked with a concerned look.

Gilbert smiled at his son. "Perfectly fine."

For a second, Ethan looked doubtful, but he was quickly drawn back into conversation as Jacob suggested drawing up a map of all the passageways they had discovered thus far. They continued discussing their plans for another few minutes, during which Elaine never once looked up, a rosy bloom warming her cheeks.

Gilbert smiled, certain of where her thoughts lingered.

"May we be excused, Father?" Ethan asked, impatience upon his face.

Gilbert nodded in acquiescence. "Good luck to you both."

The boys quickly rose from their chairs and hurried toward the door, eagerness in their voices as they planned their next steps.

"If you'll excuse me, my lord," came Elaine's voice as she, too, pushed to her feet, clearly determined to flee his presence, "but I have a few...letters to write." She was halfway to the door before Gilbert caught up with her.

"You're running away again," he remarked, not daring to reach out to grasp her arm. Something was different this morning, different from the days before. Did she have regrets?

Gilbert breathed a sigh of relief when his words gave her pause. She stopped but did not turn to face him.

"Elaine?" he asked carefully, moving closer until he stood right behind her. Her shoulders rose and fell with uneven breaths, and he thought to see a tremble in her chin as she straightened. "I missed you this morning."

Instantly, the lady whipped around, her eyes wide and her cheeks alternating between frighting paleness and mortifying crimson.

Gilbert sighed. "It seems our relationship is only capable of extremes." He shifted closer. "Either you're in my arms, your need for me as consuming as mine is for you," her eyes dropped from his, "or you're avoiding me, barely able to meet my eyes."

At his words, her eyes snapped back up to meet his.

"Why?" he asked, wishing to understand. She had felt something last night. He was certain of it. Why then did she hide from him again? "Do you...Do you have...moral objections to what happened between us last night?" he asked in a whisper. "Do you regret what we did?"

Her blush intensified, and her mouth opened and closed but no words emerged. Was she merely embarrassed?

Gently, Gilbert reached for her hand, surprised to find it chilled. "Are you all right?" he asked, pulling her closer, pleased that she allowed him. "Have you never before experienced such a night?" He dipped his head to hold her gaze as she lowered her own. "With either of your husbands or...perhaps with another, since you were widowed?"

Again, her chin shot up, her eyes wider than before, deep shock marking her features. "What are you suggesting?" she asked, taking a step away from him and retrieving her hand. "I'm not..." She swallowed, then cleared her throat. "I'm not that kind of woman. What happened last night...we..." Her chin rose a fraction. "It shouldn't have. It was a mistake."

Gilbert could see that she was about to run again, but he caught her arm before she could, bringing her close to him, closer than before. "It was not," he growled, his gaze fixed upon hers. "It was not a mistake. Far from it."

Her jaw trembled, and she pressed her lips into a tight line. "Perhaps it would be better if we left, Lord Errington. It was kind of you to invite us, but I'm afraid you might have the wrong idea of why I...of why we are here." She swallowed, fighting to hold on to her composure.

Not releasing her arm, Gilbert wrapped his other arm around her middle, holding her locked in his embrace. "Perhaps you are mistaken about my intentions."

She scoffed. "I believe you've made them unmistakably clear, my lord."

"Gilbert!" he insisted, his voice harder than it ought to be. Yet the thought of her leaving brought him to the edge of madness. She could not leave! He could not let her go!

"Please, release me, my lord," Elaine insisted, a haughty expression in the way she lifted her chin; her eyes, however, never quite met his.

Inhaling a deep breath, Gilbert complied, raking his mind for something to say, something that would convince her to stay, to admit that she had felt something. And she had, had she not? Or could he have been so severely mistaken?

Watching her walk to the door, Gilbert felt every ounce of happiness wash away. "Do I mean nothing to you?" he asked as his heart clenched painfully in his chest. "Nothing at all?"

The lady stopped once more, then slowly turned to look at him over her shoulder. "You cannot," was all she said before inclining her head to him in a gesture that seemed to imply a farewell, and then walked from the room.

Gilbert hung his head. He had been so certain that something had developed between them over the past fortnight. Slowly, but there, nonetheless. Was he simply to let her leave? With no hope for a next meeting? It was what she intended, was it not?

Still, as Gilbert walked rather randomly through Errington Hall, his legs as restless as his mind, he could not help but feel that Elaine had indeed seemed different this morning. Before, she had been uncertain, clearly surprised by his interest in her. To Gilbert, it was now clear that she had never sought to refuse his attentions, but that she had simply never realized his interest in her. She had only ever looked at him and seen Ethan's father, nothing more.

Now, however, she knew differently. She was no longer uncertain; yet if she worried about his intentions, fearful that he only intended a brief love affair, would she not have spoken her mind? Asked him to state his intentions clearly?

Instead, she seemed on the verge of fleeing his presence. Why?

Remembering the look upon her face, her eyes downcast and her expression strangely overshadowed, Gilbert could not help but think that *something else* was urging her to leave, to flee his side...even though her heart wished to stay.

Throughout the day, Gilbert continued to watch her most carefully and found his suspicions confirmed. Her demeanor spoke of sadness and regret, but a look of yearning came to her eyes whenever they beheld him. However, it was quickly chased away by a sharp lift of her chin, as though she was calling herself to reason.

And then, later that evening, Gilbert finally received his answer. It happened by sheer happenstance, and he would forever bless his stars for guiding him to her chamber that night.

Supper had been a strained affair. Even their sons had taken notice, casting confused frowns around the room, their eyes moving from their parents to each other. Yet they had said nothing.

And then Gilbert had stood outside Elaine's chamber, his hand lifted to knock when voices from inside had drifted to his ears. Fortunately for him, the door had been left ajar—by accident, he supposed—and he could clearly make out not only Elaine's voice, but also Jacob's.

"I'm sorry, Jake, but we need to leave. We'll go spend Christmas with your Aunt Elizabeth." The cheerfulness in her voice sounded forced. "You'll have your cousins to keep you company and—"

"No!" Jacob exclaimed, a deep sense of anger and confusion in that one word. "Why? At least, tell me that! Why do we suddenly have to leave?"

Holding his breath, Gilbert listened carefully.

Chapter Twelve
FOR THOSE WE LOVE

Elaine hated herself for ruining her son's Christmas. It was clear as day that leaving Errington Hall upset him deeply, and yet there was no other way.

"Why?" Jake asked again, his eyes narrowed in suspicion as he stepped toward her. "Why now? What happened?"

Elaine swallowed hard, desperately searching her mind for something to say. Anything. After all, Jacob was twelve years of age. She could not very well drag him away from Errington Hall without providing at least some sort of explanation. More than that, he deserved one.

"Is it because of Lord Errington?" Jacob asked, a look upon his young face that seemed all too knowing.

Busying her hands by brushing non-existent lint off her dress, Elaine turned away. "What makes you say that?" Her heart beat frantically in her chest as she wondered what her son might have observed between her and...Gilbert. He could not possibly know that they had...?

She shuddered at the thought.

"Because he cares for you," Jacob replied without hesitation. She heard her son move behind her, quick footsteps carrying him across the carpet and to her side before she felt his hand settle upon her arm, urging her to look at him. "Has he done anything..." a slight frown appeared upon his young face, "...untoward?"

Elaine felt ready to faint. Never in a thousand years would she have assumed to have this kind of conversation with her young son. Her jaw dropped as she tried to speak but no words came out, an affliction she seemed prone to lately.

"Mother?" Jacob pressed, deep concern in his kind eyes. "Are you well?"

Elaine nodded. "Yes, of course, I am. It is nothing. Nothing for you to worry about."

"But I am worried. Tell me what happened? Should I speak to him?"

The world around her suddenly seemed to spin, and Elaine had to reach out a hand to brace it against the wall, steadying herself. "No, there is no need. I assure you, nothing...untoward happened." Although it was odd, Elaine had never felt more like a liar than she did in that moment.

"But it has to do with him, does it not?"

Elaine offered her son what she hoped was an unconcerned smile. "What on earth makes you say that?"

For a moment, Jacob seemed to contemplate his answer, a deeply thoughtful expression in his eyes as he regarded her carefully. Then he sighed, shrugged his shoulders like someone throwing caution to the wind and said, "Because he's in love with you."

For the second time, the world seemed to turn upon its axis most unusually, spinning rather uncontrollably as her son's words continued to echo in her mind.

"Did you truly not know?" Jacob asked, a rather indulgent smile coming to his face. "I thought it very obvious. So did Ethan. He told me months ago that he believed his father in love with you. It is why we came up with this plan." A bit of a sheepish grin came to his face. "Only we sent the invitation too early. You had time to write back, which almost ruined everything. However, Ethan said that when his father found out, he approved of what we had done. He wanted you here as well."

Staring at her son, Elaine all but forgot to breathe.

"We did what we could to give you time alone," Jacob elaborated. "It seemed to work. The two of you seemed to grow closer." A frown came to his face, and his nose scrunched up slightly. "Do you not like him? I always thought you would. I just wanted to see you happy, like Juliet. I've never seen you like that. Neither has she. She told me. I spoke to her about our plan."

Feeling faint, Elaine staggered to the nearest armchair and sank down. "Your sister knew?" She swept her hand outward, indicating everything that had happened here at Errington Hall. "And she encouraged you?"

Jacob nodded. "She wants to see you happy as well. Is that so wrong? Are you not happy when you're with him?"

Elaine closed her eyes, not daring to answer, not wanting to lie again. "You are a sweet boy for doing this for me," Elaine said gently, reaching out a hand and placing it upon his cheek. "Believe me, I am most grateful and truly touched by your thoughtfulness." She swallowed, trying not to let the sorrow that rested in her heart show upon her face. "However, I have no intention of ever marrying again. There is no need for me to do so, and I do not believe it would be wise."

That all too grown-up frown came to Jacob's face once more as he contemplated her words. "Do you say so because of Father? Are you afraid Lord Errington would find out that your marriage was never valid?"

Instantly, Elaine shot to her feet, holding out her hand to quiet her son. "Please, do not speak of it. For your own sake, never ever mention it again. It could spell disaster for all of us if anyone were to find out." Of course, Elaine had never spoken to her son about the consequences for her marriage when she had learned that her husband's first wife had never passed. Yet, somehow, Jacob had found out.

Secrets did have a way of fighting to see the light of day, did they not? And she would do well to remember that.

A determined set came to Jacob's jaw as he shook his head. "Lord Errington would never think ill of you, of us. Nor would Ethan."

Elaine felt the blood drain from her face. "You did not tell your friend, did you?"

Jacob shook his head. "I did not, but I can assure you that it would not matter to them. Ethan is my friend, and he will stand with me no matter what." His shoulders drew back with pride. "And his father, he would not think any less of you. Believe me. None of what happened was your fault."

Elaine closed her eyes and sank back into the armchair. "I know that. Yet in these cases, it rarely matters whose fault it was." She reached out for his hands and held them within her own. "I cannot risk your future, your well-being, your happiness. Please, understand."

Jacob heaved a deep sigh. "You need to make your own choices, Mother, but do not forget that I could never be happy so long as you are not also."

Warmth swept through her as Elaine stared at her son, amazed by the young man he had become despite the harmful influence of his father. Indeed, she saw nothing of her late husband in Jacob. He was all goodness and kindness. He was thoughtful and compassionate, willing to go to great lengths to see those he loved happy.

Elaine swallowed, blinking back tears. Never had she been prouder.

Chapter Thirteen

IN THE DARK OF NIGHT

Sleep would not come that night. Elaine tossed and turned, unable to forget the words that had passed between her and her son. Most of all, she remembered him saying, *Because he's in love with you.*

Smiling, Elaine buried her face in her pillow, wishing Jacob's words would disappear from her memory, taking that deep longing with it. Even if it was true, even if Gilbert truly loved her, she could not risk it, could she? This was her son's future. No matter how much she wished life could be different, it simply was not. She could not be certain how Gilbert would react if she told him the truth. He might not care or...

Feeling restless, Elaine slipped from the bed and began to pace in front of the fireplace. Waves of warmth rolled toward her, touching her chilled skin, but she was unable to settle the disquiet that lingered in her body. She knew she needed to leave on the morrow, but she, also, knew she did not wish to.

Lost in her thoughts, Elaine paused when she thought she heard a soft knock. Had she merely imagined it? Then it came again, only not from the direction of the door, but from...

Elaine's breath caught in her throat as she turned to stare at the small writing desk in the corner with the wooden panel behind it. The wooden panel that hid the tunnel that led to Lord Errington's chamber.

Again, a knock echoed to her ears, beckoning her forward.

Although she knew she ought not, Elaine could not help herself. Her feet moved forward, carrying her closer and closer. Again, she pushed the small writing desk aside, her hands finding the smooth wood hiding the opening in the wall. She closed her eyes, her mind and heart warring with one another about what to do. And then her hands suddenly gave a slight push, and she heard a soft *click* drift to her ears.

Stepping back, Elaine watched the wood panel slide open. Almost entranced, she stood there, waiting, and then her eyes fell on Gilbert.

Of course, it was him. She had known it would be him the moment she had located the knock. Who else could it have been? Only why was he here? Why did he come to her? And why through the tunnel and not the door?

Slowly, Gilbert stepped out of the passageway, his eyes dark in the dim light of the room as he moved toward her. A tentative smile curled up the corners of his mouth. She could see it even though the lower half of his face lay hidden behind his beard.

"What are you doing here?" Elaine demanded, reminding herself that she planned to leave on the morrow. "You're not to be here. This is most...inappropriate."

The smile upon Gilbert's face deepened, and a suggestive gleam came to his eyes. "I have come to invite you out into the night," he replied mysteriously, the look upon his face teasing, yet insistent.

A shiver trailed down Elaine's back, and she wrapped her arms around herself, only now remembering that she wore her night rail and nothing more. "Leave! I'm not even dressed. You need to go."

Instead of complying, Gilbert took another step into her chamber, the look in his eyes telling her she would not be able to rid herself of him easily...or at all. "Then get dressed," he urged with a grin, "and dress warmly. It is freezing outside."

"Outside?"

Gilbert nodded that deeply unsettling grin still upon his face. "Out-side," he confirmed before he took that last step toward her, his right hand reaching out to grasp her chin. "You have ten minutes." His gaze remained upon hers, and her breath lodged in her throat as she felt his warm breath against her lips. "Then I will come for you, dressed or not."

As Elaine continued to stare at him, her mind as frozen in place as her body seemed to be, the corners of Gilbert's mouth twitched once before he abruptly leaned forward and pressed his lips to hers.

His mouth lingered upon hers as he pulled her into his arms; yet he did not deepen the kiss. He simply held her, and she felt the tips of his fingers brush over her right temple, then tug a stray curl behind her ear. "Ten minutes," he repeated as he pulled back, the look in his eyes telling her he meant what he said.

Then he turned and walked back the way he had come, quickly swallowed up by the darkness inside the tunnel. Belatedly, Elaine realized he had not even brought a candle.

A minute passed, in which Elaine simply stood there and stared into the blackness. Her mind felt sluggish, and she could not seem to bring herself to focus.

Ten minutes!

She flinched as Gilbert's words echoed in her head, and she quickly closed the wooden panel.

Then I will come for you, dressed or not!

Although Elaine did not know how she felt about his sudden appearance in her chamber, she was certain that he was a man of his word. He always had been. And so she rushed to dress.

And dress warmly.

Pulling on her heavy winter boots, Elaine hurried to wrap a thick woolen scarf around her neck before reaching for her winter coat. She was only just slipping it on when another knock sounded.

This time, however, it came from the direction of the door.

Quick steps carried her over, and she opened the door without another thought of hesitation. As much as she feared his attentions, his insistence, she could not help but feel excited by this sudden adventure. Indeed, Jacob had been right. Of course, he had been right. She cared for Gilbert. She did. And she loved being with him. She felt most alive when he was near. Yet...

An approving smile came to his face as his eyes swept over her.

"Well done," he remarked, then he pulled her arm through his. Without another word, he escorted her down the corridor.

"Where are we going?" Elaine whispered, hoping that they would not stumble upon anyone. Least of all, one of their sons.

Gilbert grinned at her. "You'll see." The world around them was almost pitch-black, and yet Gilbert moved with a sure-footedness that proved he had grown up in this place and knew it better than the back of his hand.

Clinging to his arm, Elaine did not know where they were or where they were going until Gilbert pushed open a familiar-looking door. "The library?" she asked, squinting her eyes into the darkness.

A faint shimmer of silver light streamed in through the tall windows, raising shadows all around her. She looked over her shoulder at the corner where a passageway led off to the drawing room. "I thought we were going outside," she murmured, unwilling to speak too loudly.

Gilbert chuckled. "We are." Holding her close to his side, he weaved his way through the rows of tall-standing bookshelves until they reached the back of the large chamber. There, he stopped in front of a random shelf and lifted a hand to grasp the sconce on the wall beside it, giving it a strong pull.

Elaine watched with wide eyes as, in the next instant, the shelf in front of them moved. Like the wooden panel in her chamber, it swung outward, and they stepped to the side to avoid its reach.

Another dark tunnel opened before them, and Gilbert led her into it without a moment of hesitation, pulling the secret door closed behind them and plunging them into a darkness that could not be more complete.

Elaine felt her heart thud wildly in her chest as her eyes became all but useless. Her hands tightened upon Gilbert's arm, and she moved closer to him.

A warm chuckle rumbled in his throat, and for a moment, he moved toward her, enfolding her in his arms. "Trust me," he murmured, his voice so close that she could feel his breath upon her neck.

"I do," Elaine whispered without thinking, surprised to realize that she had spoken the truth. A smile came to her face at the realization, and she was about to express her surprise when Gilbert's mouth closed over hers.

Holding her in a tight embrace, he kissed her thoroughly as he had that first time behind the curtain. Elaine felt her world spin yet again; only this time, she spun with it. It felt glorious and absolutely enchanting, and she wished it would never end.

When it did, though, Gilbert rested his forehead against hers and they breathed in deeply.

Together.

As one.

"Come," he whispered then, tugging her along and down the tunnel. "It's not far."

Holding tightly to his arm, Elaine let her eyes drift through the darkness, wondering how much farther it was, when Gilbert pulled to a halt. How he knew when to stop was beyond her.

A scraping sound drifted to her ears as he pushed against the wall opposite them, the one she could not see. She could hear him grit his teeth at the effort, noting the slow slide, the sound of rock on rock.

"I'm afraid I'll need my other arm," Gilbert murmured before releasing her. "Don't worry. I'll not go anywhere." Then he took a step away from her, and she imagined him pushing his shoulder against the block of granite that barred their way.

Although Elaine knew he was there, she suddenly felt uneasy, a part of her yearning to return to his arms, the safe embrace of his presence. "Do you need help?" she asked into the darkness.

"If you don't mind," came his good-natured reply before she felt his hand settle upon her arm, pulling her forward.

Her hands found the rock wall, and they pushed together. Slowly, the door moved, bit by bit, allowing a hint of light to drift into the dark tunnel through the forming gaps.

A few more shoves, and the door opened wide enough for them to step through. Gilbert went first, holding her hand as she followed.

Blinking, Elaine found herself in a dim corridor, its walls, ceiling, and floor made of rock. Wooden doors lined each side, each with a small window at the top, which was blocked by iron bars. "The...The dungeon," she gasped, and turned to look at Gilbert. "All this time, you knew there was a way? You knew where?"

Grinning, he nodded. "My brothers and I found it long ago." He chuckled. "It took us years."

"Why do you not tell them?" Elaine asked, her eyes sweeping over their surroundings. "Ethan and Jake would be so excited."

Gilbert nodded. "They would be, but, trust me, they'll enjoy it more if they make the discovery on their own." A hint of sadness lingered in his voice, and Elaine wished she could see his face better. "Come, this way."

And Elaine followed him out into a cloudless night, the full moon overhead, casting an almost magical glow over the world. Indeed, in that moment, anything seemed possible.

And perhaps it was.

Chapter Fourteen
ON THE ICE

T he snow crunched beneath their boots as they wound their way through the woods outside Errington Hall. Gilbert was glad that Elaine had heeded his words and dressed warmly, for the chilling night air stung his cheeks like little pinpricks. "It's not much farther," he told her, clasping her hand with his own. A part of him wished they were not wearing gloves, but, of course, it was necessary.

Her warm breath billowed out into the cold air, and her wide eyes swept over the ethereal light drifting through the trees up ahead.

A few more steps and they stepped out into a clearing, the bright light of the moon overhead almost blinding.

"Oh!" Elaine gasped as her eyes fell on the frozen lake only a few steps ahead, her eyes aglow with awe. He felt her hand hold his more tightly, her teeth sinking into her lower lip as a wide smile claimed her features. "This is beautiful! I've never seen anything so..." She shook her head, at a loss for words. "It reminds me of the lake my sister and I used to—" Her voice broke off as she turned to him and her eyes fell on the skates he held in his other hand.

"Would you like to try it?" Gilbert asked, delighting in the joy that stole over her face. Never had he seen her like this. Every burden, every regret and doubt had fallen from her, and her eyes gazed out at the world with an innocent joy he had only ever seen in their children.

Her eyes moved to his. "How did you know?" she breathed, then frowned. "*Did* you know?"

Gilbert nodded. "I overheard you speaking to Lady Grennell a while back. You told her how you and your sister used to skate together as children on the lake behind your family home." He pulled her toward a fallen tree by the bank of the lake and urged her to sit. "I remember the wistful look upon your face."

Tears misted her eyes as she looked at him. "That was...at least a year ago. How can you...How can you remember that?"

Swallowing hard, Gilbert set down the skates and pulled her hands into his own. "Because I love you," he told her honestly, knowing he should have done so long ago.

"Gilbert." His name fell as a gasp from her lips as tears pooled in her eyes. Her hands held his tighter, and she looked at him in a way that gave him hope. "Why did you never say anything?"

Sighing, he shrugged. "I don't know. I was a fool." He shook his head at his own stupidity, reminding himself not to let this moment slip through his fingers. "But no more. No, now, I'm saying it and you need to hear it."

Her eyes closed, and she bowed her head. "No one ever loved me," she whispered, then looked at him again. "I saw it around me, in others, even in my daughter, but I never found it myself. I never thought..." Her right hand slipped from his and she reached up to cup his face. "I think I feel it, too."

Joy almost brought Gilbert to his knees, and he briefly closed his eyes to savor the moment. "You do?"

Elaine nodded, and a tear spilled over. It trailed down her cheek, glistening in the soft moonlight. "I never noticed it before. I never... looked at you...that way before." She smiled at him. "But ever since we arrived, you've been...different. I couldn't help but look at you, see you and...it made me wonder." She shook her head. "I was so confused, and I did not know what to make of it. Of you."

"I love you," Gilbert said again, pulling her closer until she almost sat on his lap. "That is the truth." He swallowed. "What will you do with it?"

At his words, she tensed, and he could see her withdraw, her emotions held at bay by a fear that lurked in her eyes. "I...I want to, but..." She bowed her head, as though in defeat, in surrender.

"Listen," Gilbert said gently, reaching out to grasp her chin and make her look at him. "There is something I need to tell you. Something I have never told anyone." Interest sparked in her eyes. "It is a secret I've been keeping for years, one that if revealed would threaten my son's happiness, his future, everything." He swallowed hard, surprised how hard it was to speak the words. No wonder she, too, was hesitant!

As expected, Elaine's eyes grew round, shock marking her features as she waited for him to continue.

Gilbert heaved a deep breath and then forged ahead. "I told you about my wife," he began, and she nodded. "Constance and I grew up together. She was my dearest friend, and I loved her...as I would have loved my own sister." Pain burned in his chest at the memory of her loss. "One day, at a ball, I found her crying in a corner. She refused to talk to me, but eventually she gave in and told me everything." He closed his eyes, praying that Constance would not see his next words as a betrayal. "She had fancied herself in love and now found herself with child."

Elaine gasped, her hands moving to cover her mouth. Yet, the look in her eyes held compassion, not judgement.

Gilbert exhaled a deep breath, watching the puff of air drift away on the night's icy breeze. "The man she had fancied herself in love with refused to marry her. In fact, he was already engaged to another."

"Oh, dear, she had to have been heartbroken," Elaine exclaimed with a hitch in her voice, "and so very afraid." Again, she reached for his hands, her warm, brown eyes holding his. "You saved her, did you not?"

Gilbert swallowed. "I don't know if I would call it that, but, yes, I married her." He bowed his head. "And then she died when Ethan was born." Closing his eyes, Gilbert reached for Elaine the moment he felt her hands settle upon his shoulders. He pulled her into his arms, and for a long while, they clung to one another.

The pain over Constance's passing still lingered—even after all these years. Yet becoming a father had changed Gilbert's life in such a wonderful, priceless way that he did not even dare contemplate what would have been if Constance had not married him, if Ethan's true father had done the honorable thing. Gilbert had always thought himself blessed to be Ethan's father, and he could not have loved him more if the boy had been his blood.

Ethan was his son in every way that mattered.

Gilbert had always known so.

The cold lingered around them like a cloud; yet Gilbert had never felt warmer than he did in that moment. Every word that had been spoken had given him peace of mind and heart. He was holding the woman he loved in his arms—finally!—and he had hope.

"I wish to tell you something as well," Elaine whispered, her breath brushing over his ear before she pulled back and looked into his eyes. Tension stood upon her face, and her mouth opened and closed as she gathered her courage.

Gilbert smiled, seeing his wish granted. More than anything, he had wanted her to trust him with her secret, to be willing to share it with him. He needed nothing more. "I already know," he said then before she could speak.

A frown tugged down her brows. "You...? What do you mean?"

He swallowed, praying she would not hold his eavesdropping against him or even see it as a betrayal. Still, he simply could not keep this from her, let alone lie to her. "I stood outside your chamber when you spoke to Jake."

Her eyes widened, and her body grew rigid as she stared at him. "You..."

"I'm sorry," Gilbert assured her, wrapping his hands more tightly around hers. "I did not mean to listen. I came to your chamber to speak to you, to find out why you were so determined to run from me, from what we could have together." He reached out and gently cupped her face. "And then I heard you and Jacob, and...I simply could not walk away. I was afraid if I did so, I would lose you. You would leave and..." He shrugged, remembering the fear that had pulsed in his blood not too long ago.

Elaine swallowed, the urge to drop her gaze visible as her eyes looked into his. "So...you know." Again, she swallowed, and a tremble shook her frame.

Gilbert nodded. "I know, and it does not matter." He smiled at her, and she exhaled audibly. "Jacob was right about what he told you. You did nothing wrong, and none of what happened is your fault. While others might fault you for it, I would never dream of it. I swear it."

For the duration of a long, deep breath, Elaine closed her eyes, her hands holding onto his. "Thank you," she whispered then, opening her eyes again. "Thank you for...being you." She chuckled, as tears ran down her cheeks. "I cannot regret what happened all those years ago because it brought happiness to many people, including my own daughter. She would not be happily married today, would never even have met her husband if...my husband's first wife, Alexandra, had not faked her death and left him." She shook her head, a look of awe in her eyes. "Everything is connected, and we cannot know what good will come from something that at first frightens us. I can honestly say that I'm happy for her, for Alexandra, because she found someone who... who looks at her the way you...you are looking at me right now." Tears stood in her eyes as she slowly shook her head, as though fearful that the image before her eyes was nothing but a mirage. "Is it true?" she whispered and leaned closer, her deep brown eyes searching his. "Do you love me? Truly?"

Gilbert held her close. "I do," he told her with vehemence in his voice, needing her to believe him, to believe that she was worthy of love. Somehow, he thought she doubted it. "I love you, and I have for a while."

A sob escaped her lips, and she threw herself into his arms. "Oh, I love you as well. I do. I know I do, and I can finally say it. I can finally admit it to myself."

Gilbert felt a heavy weight lifted off his shoulders, off his heart. He had known, and yet he had needed her to say it. He had needed to hear it. He had never loved, either. Not like this. Not the way he loved her, and he knew precisely what to do about it. "Will you marry me?"

Instantly, her sobs quieted, and she stilled in his arms. Then, ever so slowly, she moved back until her tear-filled eyes met his. "Do you truly mean it?" She looked completely overwhelmed. Her world had turned upside down in one day, and she was struggling to get her feet back under her.

"I do," Gilbert assured her. "I want you to be my wife. I want our sons to be brothers. I want us to be a family." He smiled at her. "I want us to be happy, the way your daughter is happy with her husband and your late husband's first wife...Alexandra?...is happy as well." He grinned, amazed at how complicated and yet utterly simple life could be at times.

Elaine laughed. "Yes!" she exclaimed, nodding her head vigorously. "Yes! I want all that as well. I do!" Then she threw herself back into his arms, and they held each other until snow began to fall.

Tiny flakes drifted down from the moonlit sky, glistening in its silvery light as they settled softly on the world and made it glow. They fell on Elaine's dark blue cloak and his black coat as well as her reddened cheeks, where they melted and mingled with the tears still running down her face. Yet they were tears of joy and soon laughter joined them.

"Shall we skate?" Gilbert asked, reaching for the skates he had set aside.

"Oh, yes, please!" Elaine exclaimed, clapping her hands together like a child on Christmas morning.

Eagerly, they strapped on the skates and then carefully made their way to the frozen lake. Years had passed since either of them had last stood upon the ice. Still, only moments after pushing off from the lake's bank, it felt wonderfully familiar again.

With a bright smile upon her face, Elaine surged across the ice, sure-footed, as though she had done this every day of her life. Her cheeks shone rosy, not with mortification, but with utter delight, and Gilbert could not stop looking at her.

Long into the night, they remained upon the ice, skating arm in arm, and Gilbert could not imagine anything more wonderful. This was what he wanted, what he had wanted since the moment he had first laid eyes upon Elaine.

Sometimes one had to be patient.

Sometimes one had to fight against the odds.

And sometimes one was rewarded.

Epilogue

Errington Hall, 1814 (or a variation thereof)

Two years later

Elaine loved Errington Hall, especially in winter. With the snow covering everything, wrapping it in a white blanket, their little place of heaven seemed far removed from the rest of the world. It was as though nothing and no one else existed but them. Only snow as far as the eye could see.

"We found it! We found it!"

At the sound of the boys' voices, everyone stopped what they were doing and turned toward the door a moment before Jacob and Ethan came bursting through it.

After spending the morning outside in the snow, the family now sat huddled together in front of a roaring fire in the drawing room with an assortment of hot beverages: tea with cinnamon, hot chocolate, and warm milk for the little ones.

Roughly a sennight ago, Juliet and her family had arrived from France to spend Christmas at Errington Hall. Although France and England were still at war, as a privateer, Henri Duret knew how to find his way onto English soil undetected.

After all, to Elaine's knowledge, her son-in-law had done so before...more than once. The last time, he had whisked Juliet away to France and married her.

"*Papa! Papa!*" little Eloise cried, her right forefinger pointing at Jacob and Ethan as she tugged upon Henri's coat sleeve. At almost two years old, the little auburn-haired daredevil knew precisely what she wanted and was not afraid to demand it.

Elaine chuckled, knowing her daughter and son-in-law had their hands full with her granddaughter.

Smiling, her gaze moved across the room to the armchair by the fire where her husband sat, holding their own one-year-old daughter Constance, who slept rather peacefully despite the commotion. She was a very content baby with wide gray eyes that looked out at the world with awe and wonder...perfectly happy to sleep through most of its excitement.

"What did you find?" Juliet asked as she exchanged a look with Elaine, for mother and daughter sat side by side on the settee, enjoying a peaceful moment as their husbands doted upon their daughters.

Ethan seemed to trip over his tongue in his eagerness, his breath coming fast. "The passageway!" he panted, grinning from ear to ear—just like Jacob. "We found it!"

"The one to the dungeon!" Jacob clarified, bouncing in his step. "We found it! We found it! Come quick!" And before anything else could be said, the boys darted off, their footsteps echoing on the stone floors.

"*Papa! Vite!*" little Eloise exclaimed, still pointing at the door as she tried to climb onto her father's shoulders.

Henri laughed, abandoning their tea party on the carpet, and rose to his feet, seating Eloise securely upon his broad shoulders. "As you command, *mon général.*" Then he stepped toward Juliet and held out his hand to her. "Care to join us, *ma petite lionne?*"

Smiling, Juliet grasped her husband's hand and let him pull her to her feet. "Nothing could stop me," she whispered, and as they strode out into the corridor, they shared a look that made Elaine's gaze travel to her own husband.

Holding Constance close to his chest, Gilbert pushed out of the chair and moved toward her, his silver-gray eyes sparking with amusement. "It seems they found it after all," he laughed quietly, casting a cautious look down at Constance.

Their daughter, however, simply smiled in her sleep and snuggled closer into her father's embrace.

Elaine brushed a hand over the little girl's dark hair. "Sleep, little Connie. Sleep." She placed a quick kiss on her forehead and then smiled up at her husband. "You were right."

"Of course, I was," Gilbert agreed with a feigned look of superiority. Then he frowned. "About what?"

Elaine laughed. "About the passageway, of course. It was good that you did not show it to the boys. They had so much fun searching for it." She sighed. "They were so diligent even after two years. I never feared they would give up."

Gilbert grinned. "It took my brothers and I five years to find that particular passageway."

"Five years?" Elaine gaped at him.

He nodded, a deep sigh leaving his lips. "Those were the greatest moments of my youth." He smiled at her. "I wouldn't want to have missed them."

Elaine nodded as she looked up into his warm eyes. "Sometimes, finding what we seek might take some time, but it is definitely worth it."

Leaning down, Gilbert placed a tender kiss on her lips. Then he lifted his head and grinned. "I'll take that as a compliment."

Slapping his shoulder, Elaine tried to glare at him but failed. "Let us hurry," she said, urging him out into the corridor, "before our sons run out of patience."

As they strode along, Juliet's voice called from up ahead. "We lost them. Any idea where they went?"

Grinning, Gilbert nodded. "Follow me."

As the men moved ahead, Juliet stepped to Elaine's side and slipped her arm through hers. "Would you consider coming to visit us in the summer?"

"In France?" Elaine murmured, remembering the beautiful home of the Duret family where Juliet had gotten married. "We would love to if your husband can arrange it."

With a confident grin upon his face, Henri turned to look at her from up ahead. "*Mon plaisir*, Elaine." He gave a little bow, but he quickly turned back to the front when Eloise tugged upon his black hair and urged him onward.

A deep smile came to Juliet's face as her gaze shifted from her little family back to her mother. "I do miss you terribly, and I'm so glad we're here now." She hugged Elaine closer. "I'm overjoyed to see you so happy, Mother. I've always wanted that for you."

Elaine returned her daughter's smile. "So have I. I simply never thought it possible." She chuckled. "I've never been so happy to be proven wrong."

All together, they hurried down the corridor toward the library to be shown the boys' discovery, the sound of footsteps ringing through the halls. It spoke of life and laughter, and Elaine knew she would never take it for granted.

THE END

Have you already read Juliet and Henri's story? A French privateer and an English lady make for an adventurous love story in *Scorned & Craved - The Frenchman's Lionhearted Wife*.

Or follow Lord Silcox's first wife, Alexandra, as she stumbles over the love of her life utterly unexpectedly one night, in *Trapped & Liberated - The Privateer's Bold Beloved*.

LOVE'S SECOND CHANCE SERIES: TALES OF LORDS & LADIES

LOVE'S SECOND CHANCE SERIES: TALES OF DAMSELS & KNIGHTS

LOVE'S SECOND CHANCE SERIES: HIGHLAND TALES

THE WHICKERTONS IN LOVE

FORBIDDEN LOVE NOVELLA SERIES

HAPPY EVER REGENCY SERIES

For more information visit www.breewolf.com

About Bree

USA Today bestselling and award-winning author, Bree Wolf has always been a language enthusiast (though not a grammarian!) and is rarely found without a book in her hand or her fingers glued to a keyboard. Trying to find her way, she has taught English as a second language, traveled abroad and worked at a translation agency as well as a law firm in Ireland. She also spent loooong years obtaining a BA in English and Education and an MA in Specialized Translation while wishing she could simply be a writer. Although there is nothing simple about being a writer, her dreams have finally come true.

"A big thanks to my fairy godmother!"

Currently, Bree has found her new home in the historical romance genre, writing Regency novels and novellas. Enjoying the mix of fact and fiction, she occasionally feels like a puppet master (or mistress? Although that sounds weird!), forcing her characters into ever-new situations that will put their strength, their beliefs, their love to the test, hoping that in the end they will triumph and get the happily-ever-after we are all looking for.

If you're an avid reader, sign up for Bree's newsletter on **www.breewolf.com** as she has the tendency to simply give books away. Find out about freebies, giveaways as well as occasional advance reader copies and read before the book is even on the shelves!

Connect with Bree and stay up-to-date on new releases:

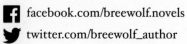

facebook.com/breewolf.novels
twitter.com/breewolf_author
instagram.com/breewolf_author
bookbub.com/authors/bree-wolf

Made in United States
North Haven, CT
11 June 2022

20109674R00059